"It was nothing."

"Not what the Bayside
men at the end of the

"Bayside Blogger said you saw your high school girlfriend and fell into the bay," added the other man.

Carissa's mouth dropped open. She'd thought someone had been around her when she'd stopped to look out over the water. Jasper had been at the dock when she'd pulled up a couple hours ago? He'd fallen into the bay? Because of her?

"Jasp—"

"Don't say anything."

She didn't know whether to laugh or cry. But she decided to give him a break since he looked so uncomfortable. "Who is this Bayside Blogger I keep hearing about?"

He looked relieved at the change in topic. "The Bayside Blogger..." He proceeded to tell her all about the town's biggest gossip columnist as they enjoyed their drinks.

"So, Carissa Blackwell..." He trailed off sometime later and met her eyes. A shadow fell over his face. "Sorry, I don't know what your married name is."

They were just finishing their second round of fried mozzarella sticks. Not to mention they'd kept the drinks flowing. Carissa felt warm and toasty. Her drive, the gossip, the Bayside Blogger, all forgotten.

Ah, she understood. "I never changed my name, actually."

SAVED BY THE BLOG: This matchmaking gossip columnist won't stop until true love wins!

Dear Reader,

Welcome back to Bayside!

Can you believe I wasn't going to write a book about Jasper Dumont? Luckily, my amazing agent, Nicole, stepped in. I think her actual words were "Are you crazy! You have to write Jasper's story." Thanks, Nic. As usual, you were right.

So I give you the younger Dumont brother's story. I hope you enjoy reading about Jasper as much as I loved writing about him. Jasper has been able to get any woman he wants. Oh...except for the one woman he *really* wants. Enter Carissa Blackwell, his first love. On the outside, Carissa may seem like she has it all, but trust me, she's been put through the wringer since high school.

What is it about reuniting high school loves? There's something ultimately romantic about that first person who got your heart beating faster.

It should be pretty interesting to watch Jasper and Carissa navigate their reunion. Not to mention that the pesky Bayside Blogger is just loving watching (and gossiping about) these two.

I hope you love *Bidding on the Bachelor* and the entire Saved by the Blog series. I'd love to connect, so please visit my website at kerricarpenter.com, or find me on Facebook, Twitter and Instagram. I promise not to bombard you with too many dog pictures. Well...maybe. ☺

Happy reading and glitter toss,

Kerri Carpenter

Bidding on
the Bachelor

———

Kerri Carpenter

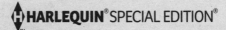

Recycling programs
for this product may
not exist in your area.

ISBN-13: 978-0-373-62379-2

Bidding on the Bachelor

Copyright © 2017 by Kerri Carpenter

All rights reserved. Except for use in any review, the reproduction or
utilization of this work in whole or in part in any form by any electronic,
mechanical or other means, now known or hereinafter invented, including
xerography, photocopying and recording, or in any information storage
or retrieval system, is forbidden without the written permission of the
publisher, Harlequin Enterprises Limited, 225 Duncan Mill Road,
Don Mills, Ontario M3B 3K9, Canada.

This is a work of fiction. Names, characters, places and incidents are
either the product of the author's imagination or are used fictitiously,
and any resemblance to actual persons, living or dead, business
establishments, events or locales is entirely coincidental.

This edition published by arrangement with Harlequin Books S.A.

For questions and comments about the quality of this book,
please contact us at CustomerService@Harlequin.com.

® and TM are trademarks of Harlequin Enterprises Limited or its
corporate affiliates. Trademarks indicated with ® are registered in the
United States Patent and Trademark Office, the Canadian Intellectual
Property Office and in other countries.

Printed in U.S.A.

Award-winning romance author **Kerri Carpenter** writes contemporary romances that are sweet, sexy and sparkly. When she's not writing, Kerri enjoys reading, cooking, watching movies, taking Zumba classes, rooting for Pittsburgh sports teams and anything sparkly. Kerri lives in Northern Virginia with her adorable (and mischievous) rescued poodle mix, Harry. Visit Kerri at her website, kerricarpenter.com, on Facebook (Facebook.com/AuthorKerri,) Twitter and Instagram (@authorkerri), or subscribe to her newsletter.

Books by Kerri Carpenter

Harlequin Special Edition

Saved by the Blog

Falling for the Right Brother

For my fabulous agent and wonderful friend, Nic.
I seriously could not do this without you.

Chapter One

Carissa could not believe this was her life.

She glanced around the nearly empty apartment—excuse her, the *luxury condo* that until recently she'd shared with her husband. Now the condo was on the market, her marriage was over, and she was left standing in a deserted room, with stacks of boxes the only thing to keep her company.

Of course, most of those boxes didn't even belong to her. As she'd packed up almost a decade of her life, she realized that she had very few belongings. Strange, since she'd been surrounded by mountains of items before she and Preston signed on the dotted line.

Even now, she took a moment to peruse the neatly packed and labeled cartons.

China—Preston's grandmother's.

Jewelry—Preston's mother's.

Antique desk—Preston's father's.

Only the kitchen gadgets and appliances, clothes, and some old high school yearbooks belonged to her now. And she didn't even want the yearbooks. She ran a hand over the maroon cover from her senior year. Good old Bayside, Virginia. Maybe she should move back home.

Carissa snorted. Yeah, right. She'd vowed to never return to Bayside, a promise easily kept after her parents moved away while she was in college. Except for her aunt Val, she hadn't stayed in touch with anyone from the town where she went to high school. Not her group of girlfriends, not her favorite teachers, not even...

"Jasper Dumont," she said aloud, and then sighed.

Her fingers itched to open the yearbook and search for his picture. She knew what she would see. His blond hair and dazzling blue eyes. That handsome face and devastating grin. They'd known each other most of their lives but for one spectacular year, they'd dated. Their relationship had been amazing and fun and passionate and...she'd gone and ruined it.

Carissa put the yearbook down. "That was a long time ago," she whispered. Ten years. A whole decade. She hadn't communicated with him since, but she did hope his life was going better than hers. She'd broken up with him and headed straight for college. Then she'd married Preston right after graduation and they'd made their life in Chicago.

We made his *life*, she thought with another glance around the room.

Even so, she did need to move somewhere. Chicago was far too expensive. As she'd quickly learned after they announced their separation, most of "their" friends turned out to really be "his" friends.

Carissa wasn't much of a crier, nor was she someone who gave in to sulking or whining. But after everything that had happened over the last year, she needed a moment. Just one moment to grieve the loss of her marriage and her life.

Maybe the problem had been marrying so young. She'd only been twenty-two when they got engaged and twenty-three when she walked down the aisle. But in her defense, she'd dated Preston all through college at Northwestern. His family had been nice and welcoming to her, and Preston graduated with an offer to work at his father's media company. That made him steady, reliable and stable.

Three traits missing from her own father, who'd barely worked a day in his life, choosing to live off her mother's inheritance instead. Well, trust funds dry up, and so did all of the promises people make to each other when they stand at the altar.

She'd worked in the beginning. Nothing fancy and not directly tied to her business degree. But she'd put in a couple years at an event-planning firm. While Carissa thought she'd done a pretty good job, her heart hadn't been in it completely. When Preston suggested she quit so she could help him entertain colleagues and clients, she'd jumped at his suggestion. She'd wanted to make him happy, and besides, she'd always loved planning meals, searching different grocery and specialty stores, puttering away in the kitchen. Watching a handful of ingredients turn into scrumptious meals with amazing aromas made her happy.

In fact, she'd enjoyed planning and hosting dinner parties so much that she'd taken countless cooking classes. Moroccan dinners, making pies from scratch, holiday baking, Italian basics…any time she got wind of any type of lesson involving food, she made sure to be the first one in line.

From Preston to his parents to all of the clients and friends they entertained, everyone raved about her cooking. Soon, she found herself enjoying the kitchen of their luxury condo much more than any other room. Including the bedroom.

Especially the bedroom.

Of course, Preston continued to adore that room. Why

wouldn't he, when he was bringing so many different women there to receive a very personal tour?

Carissa sighed and kicked one of the boxes, cringing when she heard the indelible sound of breaking glass. She checked the label and winced. Figures she'd picked one of the few boxes that held her stuff instead of the mountains of Preston's belongings.

She'd signed a prenup, which entitled her to a tiny bit of money. Apparently, the fact that Preston broke their marriage vows did nothing in the way of changing the terms. Oh well. She wouldn't want someone else's money anyway. Carissa knew she needed to move on. Now she had to figure out how, why and where.

She'd already decided that there was only one job she was qualified for. Caterer. Only, that seemed crazy. Who was she to start her own business? Sure, she'd cooked for two to fifty people multiple times a week over the last couple of years. And she did have her business degree. But she didn't have any practical experience. Not to mention references. It wasn't like she could go to Preston's clients or family and ask for their testimonials.

She also didn't have a home. She had to be out of the condo by the end of the week. It was going to be tough to cook for anyone when she didn't even have a kitchen to use.

She took another glance around the beautiful space and let out another sigh. Preston had surprised her by buying this place. At the time, she'd thought it was romantic, that Preston was taking care of her. Now those idyllic shades from her early twenties had been lifted. Her husband's buying a condo without so much as consulting with her on any aspect was controlling. Her opinion on the neighborhood had never been sought. Her name had never been added to the mortgage. The moment she'd taken the spare key from

Preston's hand had been the moment she'd lost the first part of her independence.

She heard a little chirp. Her cell phone. Someone must have left a message. She'd been so engrossed in her thoughts that she hadn't heard the phone ring.

Digging her phone out from under a mass of Bubble Wrap, packing tape and newspapers, she saw her aunt Val's name and number on the display. Carissa quickly held the phone to her ear to listen to the familiar and comforting sound of her favorite aunt's raspy voice.

Hey, gorgeous. You better not be moping in that monstrosity you call a condo. Never did like that place. Who puts marble in their bathrooms? And why do two people need four bathrooms? Anyhoo, I'm taking a little trip over the next couple of months. So if you need a place to stay, my cottage will be free.

Carissa always thought she got her strength and her levelheadedness from Aunt Val. She wasn't one for mushy scenes or histrionics and neither was her aunt. So she was surprised to hear her aunt's voice soften.

I know you have your reasons for staying away from Bayside all these years. Hell, I even understand some of them. But honey, sometimes when life kicks you in the hooha, there's no place to go but home.

Carissa didn't know whether to laugh or cry. Since she wasn't a crier and she didn't feel like laughing at the moment, she put on her thinking cap.

Never in her wildest dreams would she have imagined herself returning to Bayside. Back in high school, she'd told everyone who could listen that she was meant for bigger and better things. And those things did not include the tiny Mayberry-esque town situated on the Chesapeake Bay in Virginia. To return now, divorced, humiliated, broke, lost…well, that wasn't exactly appealing.

She crossed the room and entered the kitchen. After pouring a rather large glass of wine, she leaned back against the quartz counter she'd always loved and considered the kitchen tools she still needed to pack.

At almost twenty-nine years old, she'd been both married and divorced. She'd heeded her husband's bad advice and stopped working. She may have a college diploma, but she had no professional experience or useful contacts.

She eyed her beloved KitchenAid mixer. Cooking was the one thing she was good at. But starting a catering company in Chicago was damn near impossible on a financial level.

Bayside, on the other hand, could be doable. Many people considered Bayside to be the Hamptons of the South. The town boasted both a healthy working class and an old-school elite who lived in sprawling mansions with immaculate lawns. And the latter group loved throwing parties.

And people at those parties liked to eat.

She'd grown up as part of that upper class. The money ran out just as she reached the end of high school thanks to her deadbeat and financially challenged dad. Thank God she'd been able to keep that little secret. Small towns always seemed to have the longest memories when it came to scandals. And Bayside was a town that loved its gossip.

Carissa's heart began beating faster. She had a free place to stay, which meant she could put what little money she had into her business. If she did well, she could acquire some much-needed references. Then, if she wanted to branch out and go to DC or down into North Carolina, she could.

She took a big gulp of wine and then rubbed her hands together. Her aunt's message was exactly what she needed to hear.

Carissa still might not know the how or the why. But she finally knew the where.

Bayside, Virginia, here I come.

Here I come, Jasper thought.

After months of proposals, number-crunching, presentations, research, wining and dining, not to mention good old-fashioned face-to-face meetings, Jasper was going in for the kill. He needed Arthur Morris to agree to his terms. Since Jasper had taken over Dumont Incorporated, he'd done well. Numbers were up in all divisions, but a deal like this would really go far in persuading the board that he was the right man for the job.

He rolled his shoulders. The fact that he still had to prove his worth stuck in his craw. But Jasper wasn't one to dwell on the negative. The board wanted him to bring in more big deals. Game on.

He'd come so far. Especially considering that he wasn't supposed to be here at all. His older brother, Cam, should have been heading up the family company, but Cam had decided to buck tradition and started a construction company instead. That opened the door for Dumont child Numero Dos and Jasper had barged right through. He'd always wanted to head up the company. Unfortunately, most of his life he'd been under the impression that he would never get the chance.

He thanked Cam every day for following his heart. His brother was happy, which made Jasper extremely happy. Because he was now at the helm of Dumont Incorporated and ready to impress everyone.

"As you can see, Mr. Morris, Bayside would offer you everything you're looking for." As they walked around the waterfront, Jasper pointed out landmarks to Arthur Morris. "There's a lot of tradition in this town. When it's not the height of tourist season, there are still festivals, charity events and a lot of other town activities. We've recently built up the area to the west of the bay and put in a great park. They hold farmers' markets on Sunday and an artisan and craft fair every Saturday that brings in people from all over the state."

He noticed Arthur working his jaw and jumped in before he could object. "At the same time, Bayside is an up-and-coming hot spot according to *Virginia Magazine*. Also, the *Washington Post* recently named the town one of Virginia's best-kept secrets."

Jasper fanned his hands out in front of him and made a box to highlight the site. "Putting the apartments here is a prime location, central to the town square, shopping, nightlife. Not to mention, it's an easy jaunt to both the elementary and high school for anyone with kids." He turned and put an arm around Arthur's shoulders. "And then there's this."

Arthur nodded. "It is one hell of a view. I'll give you that."

And Jasper had timed it to make sure they got the peak sunset with its array of colors blending into the water of the bay. The docked boats were bobbing along as tourists and citizens strolled along the man-made walkway that circled a good portion of the water.

Jasper was an expert negotiator and he knew he'd made his case. Still, after he'd learned of Arthur Morris's love of crabs, shrimp and lobster, he added one last detail. "And the seafood is pretty out of this world, if I do say so myself."

Arthur turned to face him. "After the dinner we had last night, I'll agree with that." He patted his round belly. "Still full from it, but don't think that will stop me from getting more before I head out of town later tonight."

Jasper smiled, but on the inside his emotions were having a dance party. "I thought you'd like that restaurant." He'd also managed to arrange the best table, with the best view, and had the chef prepare a special menu just for them. That was a definite perk that came with the Dumont name.

"Listen, kid," Arthur began, and Jasper folded his arms in front of him, intent on the next couple of sentences. "This has been a great pitch. But honestly, it comes down to the other numbers you put together for me. After that amazing dinner, I studied every sheet cover to cover. The prices you're offering go a long way and I think the return on investment is worth the risk."

Jasper nodded, reining in his excitement. He'd been working on this deal for two years and he wasn't going to rush now.

"So I'm saying yes," Arthur finished after what felt like ten minutes of silence.

"Great to hear it, sir." Jasper shook his hand and continued to play it cool. "We're thrilled to welcome a Morris complex to Bayside."

They spoke about a couple other details for the next several minutes as they walked toward Mr. Morris's rented car. Before he could drive away, Jasper had to know one thing.

"One last question. What made you say yes?"

Mr. Morris nodded as if he'd been expecting this very question. "Your father met with me regularly over the years. He gave me some great pitches."

"And yet you never said yes."

"He nagged me the same way you did, that's for sure." His smile came fast and brief. If Jasper had blinked, he'd have missed it. "But you went the extra mile."

"By plying you with the best seafood on the East Coast."

"By showing me the town. Really showing me. You love Bayside. That came across clear as day. I feel like I know the people who live here. They're not just numbers and stats in a spreadsheet. That made my decision easy."

Now it was Jasper's turn to smile. Only he held it in. He kept his usual calm business face.

"I have to say, though, I used to hear stories about you. Heard you were quite the little party kid back in the day. Weren't we all as teenagers? Happy to see you've grown out of it." Then he shook Jasper's hand, got in the car and drove away.

Only when he knew he was completely alone did Jasper let the grin out. And a fist pump for good measure.

Today is a good day. Jasper could feel the spring in his step as he made his way toward the center of the town and The Brewside Café, the addictive coffeehouse he frequented on a daily basis. While he walked, he took in the town he'd lived in for most of his life.

He'd always loved Bayside. He'd only left for college, business school and a couple years of working for another company to gain credentials. All that time, he'd missed the large bay with boats of varying sizes going in and out, the picturesque town square with the identical white siding and inviting blue awnings and shutters.

He reached for his phone and quickly scrolled through some text messages before seeing Simone's name. He grinned. Simone Graves was a feisty little redhead he'd been noticing at the gym for the last couple of months. She liked to go to Zumba classes and Jasper enjoyed seeing her shimmy around the room in her tight-fitting clothing. He'd finally asked her out, but they hadn't set a date and time yet.

Up for a drink tonight? he wrote to her.

It only took a minute for her to write back.

Wish I could. Stuck at work. This was accompanied by multiple sad emoji. But she proposed a different night to meet and Jasper accepted.

Whistling, he continued toward The Brewside. But before he entered the coffeehouse he decided to take a moment. So he changed course and headed toward the water, Mr. Morris's parting words ringing through his head.

I used to hear stories about you. Heard you were quite the little party kid back in the day. Happy to see you've grown out of it.

Well, he had been a lover of parties and the original good-time boy. But he'd also been just that—a boy. A kid. A teenager who'd been told from birth that his older brother would take over the family business. Sure, he'd been expected to work for Dumont Incorporated but he'd never been groomed to be in charge.

After all, he was the "second" son, after Cam. Overlooked and undervalued at every turn. His mother had always said he was the most good-natured child she'd ever seen. Jasper liked to think he'd held on to that his whole life. He enjoyed seeing the glass as half-full, excelled at finding the positive. He'd never harbored jealousy toward his big brother. In fact, he'd worshipped Cam. Still, being the younger child had hurt. So he'd lived it up in high school. Why wouldn't he? He knew he'd get into a good college thanks to his parents' connections. Likewise, he knew he'd be employed after college.

But as Mr. Morris said, he'd grown out of it. He'd been forced out of it, really.

Thanks to Carissa.

At the mere thought of her name, Jasper halted. Standing on the dock, he looked out at the bay, gripping the railing hard.

When was the last time he'd allowed himself to think about Carissa Blackwell? He shook his head.

Oh please. You think about her all the damn time.

Of course he did. She'd been the single most beautiful female he'd ever laid eyes on. She'd also been his first love. And with one cutting remark after graduation, she'd changed the course of his life.

Like most of the kids from his graduating class, they'd all known one another since birth. Bayside was a small town. About 90 percent of the classmates he walked with to "Pomp and Circumstance" at eighteen had been in his nursery school class, too. Carissa was no exception.

They'd continued to run in the same crowd throughout high school. They had both been popular. They were both involved in sports—he in baseball and she in cheerleading. Their parents had been friends and enjoyed the same kind of lavish lifestyles. They'd even lived on the same street.

But they hadn't crossed that line of romance until the summer before senior year.

Jasper turned and gazed toward the beach. It had happened over there. Down on the sand after one of the town's big festivals. A bunch of kids had built a bonfire. They'd both been hanging out, having some beers. Carissa used to drink wine coolers, he thought with a laugh.

Jasper started walking toward that spot on the beach. He'd always thought she was gorgeous. Who hadn't? She was like the quintessential California girl come to the East Coast with her long legs, golden skin, perfect pink lips and full blond hair that fell halfway down her back. Plus, she had those really intriguing gray eyes. To this day, he'd never seen eyes quite like hers.

That night she'd been wearing sexy jean shorts and a little red tank top. They'd shared a glance, then a head nod. Next thing he knew he was sitting next to her on a log sharing her s'more. Didn't take long for them to move their party of two farther down the beach where they'd shared one hell of a make-out session.

Just like that, they'd become hot and heavy and completely inseparable during senior year. Until about a month after graduation. Carissa had been accepted to Northwestern and he was going to UPenn, just like his father. He could never think of Carissa without his mind going to that last fateful conversation.

"Jasper, you aren't serious about anything."

"What are you talking about? I'm serious about you."

She shook her head. "That's not enough. You party all the time with your friends."

"So what? And anyway, they're your friends, too."

"I know. But I'm just saying that there's more to life than keg parties in the woods and making out in some-one's basement."

"I think we did a little more than make out."

She pointed at him. "See, you can't even be serious now. Just like my dad," she said under her breath.

"I know you're upset because your parents want to move away from Bayside..."

"That doesn't bother me. I want them to move away, actually."

"Why?"

"Never mind, that's not the point." She flung her long hair over her shoulder.

"Okaaaayyyy." He would never understand girls. "Then, what is the point?"

"You are relying on your parents' money and connec-tions to get you through life. You have no ambition and no drive. Do you think I want to be with someone like that? I don't." She looked at the ground.

He felt like someone had slapped him across the face. "What are you saying?"

"I don't want to ever come back to Bayside. I'm so done with this town. I want someone who has goals and like, initiative and stuff," She bit her lip. Even as she insulted

*him, there was sadness in her eyes. "I'm sorry, Jasper.
You just don't."*

With that, she'd walked away with his heart.

He'd tried to call her but she'd never answered. Her parents said she went to a prefreshman-year program at Northwestern. She'd wanted to get a jump on classes. Then her parents had moved away later in the year and she didn't have a reason to return to Bayside anymore. He never saw her again.

It was Jasper's nature to find a bright side. But in truth, Carissa's words stung. Not only did she break up with him, but she insulted his very character.

It had taken some time. A lot of time. But eventually, the memory of Carissa's words had kicked his butt into gear. She wanted someone with ambition and that's what he'd decided to give her. Even if they weren't actually together.

His father's name may have gotten him into college, but he worked his butt off once he got there. He joined a fraternity but when it was time for midterms or finals, he'd camp out at the library to make sure he kept his GPA up, finally graduating with honors. He never told his parents about applying to grad schools so they couldn't influence the process.

He'd come a long way from the irresponsible, somewhat reckless, carefree kid who was always the life of the party. Some people had called him foolish, but in Jasper's mind he'd always been underestimated.

At some point, though, all the hard work stopped being just for her. He'd become obsessed with doing the very best he could and in the process he'd become the head of Dumont Incorporated. If Carissa were here maybe he'd thank her. Especially after his victory tonight. But the odds of ever seeing Carissa Blackwell in Bayside again were slim to none.

His phone made a little ding alerting him to a text message. He looked down to see his brother's name. How'd it go with Morris?

Jasper began texting back but something caught his attention. Out of the corner of his eye he saw a woman standing at the same location where he'd been before his little walk down memory lane. Fingers still poised over the keypad on his phone, he didn't have time to text Cam back before his brother added, Either way, come over tonight. Let's hang out and watch the game.

Again, he began typing a reply but the woman reached her arms above her head and stretched. She was really beautiful. He peered closer and got a chill up the back of his neck.

She looked familiar. Too familiar. Jasper gripped his cell harder and began walking faster. Closer. But as he rounded the corner, she was heading away from the dock toward a black car.

He would know that sashay of hips anywhere. After all, the last time he'd seen a movement like that had been her swaying body walking away from him.

No way. No freaking way.

"Carissa?" he said into the silence around him. Luckily, no one was there to hear him talking to himself. Likewise, no one was there to see him step to the side to ensure he was actually seeing his first love and not some late-summer apparition brought on by too much work. In any case, he slipped, hit the railing with too much momentum, and before he could say *Carissa is back in Bayside*, he'd fallen over the metal divider and into the bay.

Chapter Two

Greetings, dear readers! After a brief hiatus, your ever-faithful Bayside Blogger is back from a much-needed summer vacay! And color me shocked, surprised and downright confused. Carissa Blackwell, former Bayside High A-list superstar, has also returned to our fair shores! And just why is little-miss-too-good-for-good-ole-Bayside back in town?

Let's get down to it, folks—the far more interesting question is…how does Jasper Dumont feel? Well, I understand he took a late-evening swim in the bay after catching a glimpse of his long-lost prom queen. And let's just say that the swim wasn't exactly planned…

Jasper needed some liquor.

Once he was home, freshly showered and in dry clothes, he crossed the room to the wall that held a floor-to-ceiling bookshelf. He scanned the bottom shelf until he found what he was searching for. His high school yearbook. Jasper grabbed it from the shelf, made a cup of coffee and started riffling through the pages until he got to the B names.

There she was. Carissa Blackwell. Jasper didn't need to ogle the photo to recall that long golden hair, legs that went on for miles and flawless skin that always looked like it was kissed by the sun.

Flipping more pages, he eyed the photos of the cheerleaders. There she was again, all decked out in that appealing little uniform. His lips quirked. Damn, he'd loved watching her cheer at football games. He'd loved making out with her under the bleachers after the game even more.

They'd done everything together senior year. Until she'd broken up with him. Jasper could feel his eyebrows growing close together just as something fell out from between the pages of the yearbook. A picture of the two of them at prom. He couldn't remember who had snapped it. But in the photo they were dancing; Carissa was staring up at him adoringly as he had his arms wrapped tightly around her.

To this day, Jasper still wondered what had changed. Prom had been one month before she'd dumped him. When had she stopped looking at him like that and decided he hadn't been good enough for her?

His phone—which luckily had fallen from his hand and landed safely on the dock—rang.

"Hey, Cam," he greeted his big brother.

"So?"

Jasper shifted in his seat. So what?"

"So what have you been doing?"

Jasper eyed the garbage can, where he'd decided to throw his clothes out after he climbed out of the bay. As he'd hoisted himself back onto the wooden dock, he'd snagged his pants. The quick jaunt from the water to his new condo in the center of town had been interesting. Wet and interesting. If his brother found out about it, he'd never hear the end of it.

So he decided to play it cool. "I haven't been doing anything," he lied. He paced the length of the living room. He loved this condo with its exposed beamed ceiling, brick walls and amazing view of the bay. Although, the sight of the water at the moment made him cringe.

"What do you mean you haven't been doing anything? Wasn't your huge meeting with Mr. Morris today? I've been texting you for the last hour."

Jasper snapped out of his Carissa-focused stupor. "Right. Sorry." He proceeded to tell Cam all about the meeting. His brother seemed ecstatic for him.

"That's amazing, Jasp. Congratulations."

"Thanks, Cam." And he meant it. He'd always idolized his older brother and Cam's approval meant the world to him.

"Now, what about after the meeting?"

"What do you mean?" Jasper asked hesitantly.

"I heard you celebrated by going for a little swim in the bay."

Jasper ground his teeth together. "How did you…" He trailed off. Of course, he already knew the answer to that question. How did anyone in Bayside know anything? The ever-loving, always-gossipy Bayside Blogger, of course.

The Bayside Blogger wrote for the *Bayside Bugle*'s Style & Entertainment section. No one knew her identity, or how she always—and it truly felt like always—found out the gossip before anyone else. She also utilized a daily blog, Twitter, Facebook, Instagram and just about every other form of communication in existence.

"And the Blogger said that Carissa Blackwell is back in town," Cam was saying. "She alluded to your little dip in the water having something to do with a Carissa spotting."

Spotting? When had his brother become TMZ? Time to call him out. "I thought you didn't read that…what did you used to call it? Trash, I believe," Jasper said.

Cam coughed. "Uh, Elle reads it. I just happen to catch snippets here and there."

"Sure, sure. *Elle* reads it. Doesn't explain how you would know about me falling into the bay today, though, since your beloved is out of town checking out that up-and-coming artist for the gallery. You must be losing your mind without your better half around." Got him.

Since Elle returned from living in Italy last spring, she and his brother had been practically attached at the hip. Jasper was happy for his brother. And jealous, if he was being honest. The guy was head over heels in love. And Elle looked at him the way Carissa gazed at him in that old prom photo.

"She'll be back tomorrow afternoon. Listen, Jasp," Cam said, his voice growing serious.

Here we go, Jasper thought. He knew exactly where this was heading. This was so not going to be fun.

"Yes?"

"Carissa." Cam said her name the way one might say *cancer* or *terrorist*.

"Was my high school girlfriend."

"She was way more than that and we both know it. And she's back in town."

Jasper ran a hand through his hair in frustration. "We don't know that."

"The Bayside Blogger said—"

"So what? Just because the Bayside Blogger—"

This time Cam cut him off. "Hate to admit it but the Bayside Blogger—whoever he or she may be—does tend to be right."

"It doesn't matter." Cam started to say something so

Jasper quickly beat him to the punch. "We dated a million years ago. I heard she got married and was living in the Midwest somewhere. I, on the other hand, have a date lined up with a certain hottie from the gym."

There was a long pause. "Do you want to come over?" Cam finally asked.

What he wanted was to forget that he'd seen Carissa Blackwell. He wanted to have a couple beers, be alone with his thoughts, and not hear about the damn Bayside Blogger.

Luckily, he knew just where to accomplish everything he needed. The Rusty Keg, an old dive bar, sat on the outskirts of town. People would recognize him there but they'd also give him room and leave him alone.

"No, I'm good. Honestly," he assured his brother.

And he would be. So long as he didn't see Carissa Blackwell again.

And he stayed away from water.

Carissa was not a suspicious person. She was rooted in the here and now and considered herself rational and practical. And yet she couldn't shake the feeling she was being watched.

She'd left Chicago yesterday, stayed overnight in Ohio, driven all day, hit some nasty traffic, and drunk about fifteen coffees before finally arriving in Bayside. Needing a moment to stretch—not to mention, take in the town she hadn't laid eyes on in over a decade—she'd pulled over at the dock before she made her way to her aunt's cottage.

It was while she was there, taking a moment to refamiliarize herself with Bayside, stretching and getting the kinks out of her tired muscles, when she started to get that spooky feeling. First, goose bumps broke out on her skin. Then she thought she saw someone out of the corner of her eye, over to her right. Fed up, she'd left the dock and returned to her car. That's when she'd received full confirmation that she was indeed being watched. About five people stood outside the town's popular square, staring and pointing at her while they whispered to each other and tapped away on their phones.

Great. Back in Bayside for five minutes and the welcome committee was already starting with the gossip. She wondered how long it would take for the whole town to know she'd returned. They wouldn't know she'd come home with her tail between her legs. Not as long as she could help it.

She hightailed it to her aunt's cottage in record time.

She found the key where Aunt Val had instructed her to look, in the flowerpot around back. She peered closer. A flowerpot that appeared to be holding a weed plant if she wasn't mistaken. Given that, she wasn't sure if she was excited or nervous about what she might find inside.

Carissa let herself into the two-bedroom cottage, flicked the light switch and smiled. It was the same cozy and eccentric home she remembered from high school, maybe with a few more knickknacks collected over the years. Every room was painted a different pastel color. The kitchen wasn't the most updated she'd ever seen but it was definitely workable. And bonus, it overlooked the deck, the small backyard and the bay beyond that. The view was probably worth more than the entire rest of the house.

The decor was beachy and comfortable, the exact opposite of the modern high-rise she'd shared with Preston in Chicago. Perfect. Two minutes in this place and she already felt more at ease than she had in six years in her condo. This place screamed for you to kick off your shoes, whip up a margarita and blast some Jimmy Buffett from the radio.

Carissa nodded definitely. "This will do just fine," she murmured to herself. She saw a long note on the counter and quickly scanned it. Her aunt explained the AC system, which apparently went on the fritz from time to time. Great—since it was the last week of August, the temperature in Virginia was sweltering.

She also left instructions for watering her eclectic—and hopefully legal—garden out back. There were notes about the proper remote for the television, what days the trash was picked up, and a large warning for her *not* to enjoy the absinthe in the liquor cabinet. But everything else was hers to use, borrow and enjoy.

Carissa spent the next hour hauling her boxes from the car and getting settled. Her suitcases went into the guest bedroom she would be using. A bedroom, she noted, that was decorated in an explosion of peach paint and shell tchotchkes. It was kind of like sleeping in *The Golden Girls* house but Carissa couldn't complain. The rent was free and she would be able to catch her breath.

Her parents had never liked this house. They'd claimed her aunt had too much crap and the interior decorating was childlike and outdated. But Carissa had always loved coming over to visit Aunt Val. She didn't have to worry if she spilled crumbs on the floor or made her bed. Living in her childhood home had been like growing up in a museum. The floors had been hard and the furniture uncomfortable. Forget eating anywhere but the kitchen or dining room. And a cleaning lady came through twice a week.

How'd that work out for you, Mom and Dad? Carissa shook her head. Her parents had lost all of their money and most of their stuff. Her dad had lost the money, she corrected. Not that it had been his to begin with. Her mother had come from a wealthy family with old money, which her dad had misspent, mismanaged and eventually blown through.

She didn't quite feel like unpacking yet so she meandered into the kitchen for a snack. Aunt Val said she would provide some munchies to get her started. Carissa eyed the weed plant out the sliding glass door as she recalled the use of the word *munchies*. But when she started hunting through the cabinets and fridge, there wasn't so much as a bag of chips to be found. There was another note attached to the fridge with a magnet shaped like a starfish.

Didn't have time to go to store. Sorry, Dollface.

Well, that explained that. There was a calendar hanging on the wall next to the fridge. She sighed. Just what she needed to see. A visual reminder of what today was.

Happy birthday to me.

Happy birthday to me.

Happy birthday dear recently divorced, almost completely broke twenty-nine-year-old meceeeee.

Happy freaking birthday to me.

As part of her practical nature, Carissa never needed or wanted a big party, lots of presents or any kind of fuss made over her birthday. But even she hated the fact that she'd spent the first day of the last year of her twenties driving hundreds of miles because she'd just gotten divorced. Twenty-nine years old and already she'd been both married and divorced. Not exactly the path she'd envisioned for her life.

Snagging her car keys and shaking off the morbid mood, Carissa headed out the door toward the grocery store for a few essentials: coffee, milk, bread, peanut butter and alcohol. Lots and lots of alcohol. But since there was a nice breeze, she decided to forgo the car and walk to the store instead. After the long drive, she could use the exercise.

Once at the store, she steered her shopping cart down one aisle after another, unsure of what she was in the mood for. She grabbed cereal and some snacks, a couple bags of fruit and the ingredients for chocolate chip cookies. A little birthday present to herself. But as she perused the different brands of coffee, she couldn't help but tune in to someone else's conversation. In fact, a couple different snippets of conversations. All about her.

I'm not making this up. It was her. Carissa Blackwell.

Didn't you read the Bayside Blogger's tweets today? She already knows about this.

...can't believe she's back here! Didn't she swear off Bayside back in high school?

Strange that no one ever heard from her parents again. It's like they disappeared into thin air.

Carissa checked the time on her phone. Two hours. That was all it had taken for her to become the topic of hot gossip. And who was this Bayside Blogger who seemed to know her every move?

Didn't matter. Enough of this. She needed to get outside, stat. She pushed her cart to the side, items completely forgotten, and exited the store.

All she wanted was to escape the gossips and get some air.

As she walked along the back streets of the neighborhood back toward the cottage, she remembered something. There was a dive bar that used to sit back this way. She could go for a drink. Or two.

While she headed in the direction of the bar, one of the gossipers' words reverberated through her head. *Can't believe she's back here.*

Carissa kicked at an imaginary stone. "Yeah, that makes two of us," she muttered.

Then, like a beacon calling her home, she saw the old bar at the end of the street, surrounded by a small parking lot full of stones and overgrown trees. Score. She definitely wouldn't be recognized here. Double score. Carissa knew if she filled in the gaps on the half–burned out neon sign hanging above the door, she'd read the name, The Rusty Keg.

True, she'd come out for a snack. But bars had snacks. Even more importantly, bars had alcohol. And nothing was going to make this nightmare of a day better than some good old-fashioned liquor.

She pushed open the creaky door and was immediately assaulted by a musky smell of cheap beer, fried food and sweat. The place was dark, dank and completely off the beaten path.

In other words, it was perfect.

Carissa strolled up to the bar, noticing the scratched-up wood just waiting to give someone a splinter. She reached under the bar, feeling around for a purse hook, then immediately snatched her hand back. Had she just touched someone's used wad of gum? *Yuck.* She shook her head. An establishment with a half-lit, crooked sign above the door outside and a rotting bar with mismatched bar stools that probably hadn't been cleaned since the nineties was definitely not going to have purse hooks. They probably didn't even have pinot noir. She slid a glance toward the single-stall bathroom and scrunched her nose. Forget about toilet seat covers. That was probably a mere pipe dream.

"What can I get you?" a burly man with a full *Duck Dynasty*–worthy beard bellowed from behind the bar.

"Shot of tequila and the local beer on tap."

He nodded, pulled her beer, poured the shot, but otherwise stayed silent. Carissa didn't waste any time. "Happy birthday to me," she said to no one in particular before throwing the shot back. The liquid burned her throat and made her eyes water. She turned her head and let out an exasperated "wowza" just in time to see none other than Jasper Dumont sitting right next to her, an unreadable expression on his face.

"Oh." It was all she could think to say aloud. On the inside, however, there was a whole vocal party happening. *No-freaking-way-it's-your-ex-boyfriend!*

No, not just an ex-boyfriend. Jasper Dumont was so much more than a simple ex. With some age and perspective, she realized their one-year relationship was such a short period of time in the grand scheme of life. But damn, that one year had been nothing short of amazing. Making out, dances, football games, making out, skipping school occasionally, making out, one epic prom, passing notes in calculus class, wanton looks by the lockers and even more making out. Well, making out that quickly led to much-less-PG versions of mere kissing.

Now this boy—er, man—whom she hadn't seen in a decade, but whom, if she was being brutally honest and the tequila was already loosening her up on that score, she'd never stopped thinking about was sitting right next to her. At a dive bar in her hometown.

"Carissa Blackwell," he said, his voice smooth and cutting. "Pigs must be flying because here you are. Back in Bayside."

Despite the coldness coming off him in waves, he looked amazing. Same blond hair and striking blue eyes. But that lanky boy she used to kiss under the bleachers was now all filled out with broad shoulders and from what she could see, an impressive chest. She leaned back in her chair and took a sip of her beer. More to give herself a moment and to slow down the pulse that Jasper had sent soaring.

"Miracles can happen," she said, raising her mug of beer in a toast.

"Apparently." His gaze drank her in from the top of her head over her navy blue tank top and down her capri jeans to the toes that desperately needed a pedicure. Toes that curled as he gave an appreciative nod.

"It's, um, nice to see you, Jasper." She pushed her hair over her shoulder. "I wouldn't expect to find you in a bar like this."

"Likewise," he quickly said. "Actually I wouldn't expect to find you anywhere in the city limits."

She nodded. She probably should have expected that from him. But what was she supposed to say? The truth? *I got divorced. I have no money or career and this was the only place I had to go.*

"Touché," she said instead. "But I'm back in town."

"For how long?" he asked quickly, too quickly. In fact, if she wasn't mistaken, anger laced his question. She must have reacted to it because his features softened. "Sorry, it's none of my business. And I do remember that today is your birthday. So happy birthday, Carissa."

"Thanks," she said, and meant it. She decided to offer an olive branch because the truth was that she'd dumped him and she hadn't been kind about it. This icy reception she was receiving was well deserved. While she knew the reasons behind her decision, she'd never let Jasper in on it. She'd been a bratty, selfish teenager, not capable of understanding her emotions. Unwilling to admit that Jasper had always reminded her of her father and that summer her dad had dropped a bombshell on her.

"I don't know how long I'll be in town. I'm sort of in a transition period right now." He waited patiently. After another long drink of beer, she finished. "I just got divorced." Saying the words out loud left an awful taste in her mouth. An acidic aftertaste of yuckiness.

First, shock flashed on his face. Then true concern shone in his eyes. "I'm sorry," he said.

And that might have been her undoing. Because he had every reason to be stiff and awkward with her. Instead, any kind of compassion from him loosened her lips.

"Today is my twenty-ninth birthday. I'm having a beer next to my ex-boyfriend, who hates my guts, in a dive bar in the town I swore I would never step foot in again. An ex-boyfriend I should really apologize to because I was an evil witch to him." The words were flying now. She gripped her hand tightly around her glass. "I'm not even thirty and already I've been married and divorced. And I got divorced because he freaking cheated on me."

She couldn't miss the way Jasper's eyes narrowed, his hands curled into fists, and there was a definite tic in his clenched jaw. "He cheated on you?"

"Yep. Apparently, the fact that I was homecoming queen, prom queen and head cheerleader did nothing to impress him. Or keep his pants zipped up when anyone wearing a skirt in the Central Time Zone walked by. That probably makes your whole day, doesn't it?"

He slammed his hand on the bar and she jumped. But she just as quickly composed herself. "What? You have every right to revel in my misery after the way I broke up with you. I got divorced. You win."

His eyes narrowed. "I don't want to win at that game. And I certainly don't want to hear that some idiot cheated on you. I'm sorry you're getting divorced."

"That makes one of us." With that she chugged the rest of her beer and let her head drop onto the bar. Then she remembered the threat of splinters and lifted her face back up, the tequila and beer rushing to her head.

"Water over here, please," Jasper called to the bartender. "Two waters, a basket of mozzarella sticks, and…" He looked to her.

"More alcohol," she called out weakly.

He chuckled but also reached for her hand. As he squeezed her fingers a jolt of awareness traveled up her arm. It was a sensation she hadn't felt in years. In fact, she'd never felt it with her ex-husband. Not once. Only Jasper made her toes curl, sent electric shocks to the system, and caused her stomach to flip over.

Jasper leaned back. "I don't want to talk about our past. Not tonight."

"But you're still mad."

He nodded. "Wouldn't you be?"

She couldn't argue with that.

He seemed to be considering something. Finally, he said, "I have a better idea. Like I said, I don't want to talk about our history right now. Instead, let's call a truce and be friends for the night."

Chapter Three

"Feeling better?"

She turned to Jasper. The fried cheese sticks and water went a long way to making her feel better. So did the friendship, even if it was only temporary. Jasper listened as she mumbled into her breaded mozzarella.

"Much. Thank you."

He was looking at her with an expression that she couldn't decipher. "What?" she asked.

"I'm not gonna lie," he said with total confidence in his voice. "I've thought about seeing you again since that summer. But never in my wildest dreams would I have imagined I'd run into you at a hole-in-the-wall bar of all places."

"Would it have made it any less awkward if we'd met behind the library? I seem to remember spending a lot of time with you there." Her traitorous eyes flickered down to his lips.

"Well, I remember spending a lot of time with you in my car, in my basement..."

"All those times you sneaked into my room after my parents went to sleep," she added.

"And one epic moment in the middle of the football field."

She covered her face with her hands. "Ohmigod! I can't believe we did that. What were we thinking?"

He let out a sound that was purely male. "I know what I was thinking." He wiggled his eyebrows. She wondered how one man could manage to look both adorable and sexy at the same time.

She leaned forward. "I was never thinking. Not when you were around." And wasn't that the problem? No one else in her life had been able to make her lose her train of thought. Even now, she could get lost in those mesmerizing baby blues. Which was why she needed to take a step back. But with their closeness it was hard. So she sat back in her chair, flung her hand in the air to signal the bartender.

Jasper's brow shot up. "Another one?"

"I'm twenty-nine. I'm divorced. And I'm thirsty."

His gaze roamed over her again and his eyes darkened. "Yeah, I'm thirsty, too."

God, she wanted to kiss him. Luckily, she was saved by the bell when George, otherwise known as the burly, bearded bartender, strolled over. "Still dating that little brunette from the next town over?" he asked Jasper.

"Maria? From the ice-cream place?" Jasper asked.

"No, the other one. The one who always has part of her hair in a braid," George said, pointing to the braid in his own long hair that was tied back with a red bandanna.

"Oh, you mean Julie." Jasper shook his head. "No, that's over."

Carissa raised her eyebrow. She couldn't help it. Same old Jasper apparently. Except for the year they'd dated, he'd always been a ladies' man. Not that she could blame him now. After all, he was gorgeous, young, successful. Why wouldn't he be the toast of the town? And yet this conversation was leaving a very unsettled feeling in the pit of her stomach.

George placed a large mug of beer in front of Jasper, who offered a questioning look. "It's on the house," George said. "Despite your active and envious dating life, thought you could use a pick-me-up after your little spill into the bay earlier today." With that, he turned and headed toward two older men, more than likely local fishermen if she had to guess, sitting at the end of the bar. They nodded at Jasper and started snickering.

"You fell into the bay?" she asked Jasper.

"It was nothing."

"Not what the Bayside Blogger is saying," one of the men at the end of the bar offered.

"Bayside Blogger said you saw your high school girlfriend and fell into the bay," added the other man.

Carissa's mouth dropped open. She'd thought someone had been around her when she'd stopped to look out over the water. Jasper had been at the dock when she pulled up a couple hours ago? He'd fallen into the bay? Because of her?

"Jasp…"

"Don't say anything."

She didn't know whether to laugh or cry. But she decided to give him a break since he looked so uncomfortable. "Who is this Bayside Blogger I keep hearing about?"

He looked relieved at the change in topic and proceeded to tell her all about the town's biggest gossip columnist as they enjoyed their drinks.

"So, Carissa…" He trailed off and his eyes met hers. A shadow fell over his face. "What happened, Car? I mean, what really happened between you and the man you married?"

Car. No one had called her that in ten years. Such a simple little nickname, and yet it had a huge effect on softening her heart.

She didn't know if it was the use of *Car* or the alcohol or the stress of the last couple of months. But something had her turning toward her first love and spilling everything.

"We met in college. We got married shortly after that. We lived in Chicago."

He waited. "And?"

"And what?"

He chuckled. "Come on, Car. That's nothing. I could have found out more information from Twitter."

She relented. "Fine. Our marriage was good. At first." She twisted her empty shot glass around in circles. "But Preston started working longer hours, taking more business trips."

"Uh-oh," Jasper said.

"I knew he was cheating on me. I don't know how long I knew. Only that I didn't really want to admit it. But when I found him in our newly purchased California king bed with someone, I knew keeping up the pretense of a perfect marriage wasn't going to be possible." And still, she hadn't been the one to file for divorce. Pathetic. But she kept that to herself.

"Why did you marry him in the first place?"

Because he was an escape. Because he was ambitious and driven. In other words, because he was the polar opposite of her father. Of course, she didn't dare tell Jasper that, either.

"It's a long story," she said, in lieu of the truth.

"Okay, then let me ask a simpler question. Where did you work?"

She took a long pull of her beer and wished like hell that was a simple question. "Nope." He raised a brow. "I didn't work."

His mouth fell open. "You? You didn't work. You, the queen of 'have ambition, get some drive and determination.' Little Miss 'why don't you have goals, Jasper?' did not actually have a job?"

When he put it like that…

"You've gotta be kidding me." Jasper ran a hand through his thick hair, clearly exasperated.

Her cheeks were heating up and she knew it had nothing to do with the alcohol or the stuffy bar. She didn't mean to get defensive when she said, "I mean, I did work at an event-planning firm. For a few years."

"Before you quit to be a stay-at-home wife?" He held up his hands in surrender. "I'm not judging you or anyone else for staying at home. I'm just completely confused given the last conversation we had before you left Bayside."

God, she'd been such a brat to him that day. Briefly, she considered telling him about her parents. Revealing why she'd acted so drastically and broken up with him. But he jumped in with a question.

"What are you going to do now?"

She paused for a long moment before answering. "Become a caterer. At least, I hope so."

"Seriously?"

Was it just her or had he moved closer? She could smell his cologne, a clean, crisp scent that wrapped itself around her, making the dirty bar and stale alcohol smell slide away into the background.

"Sure," she said, her voice breathy. "I love to cook, and I was the queen of the dinner party back in Chicago."

"You have experience as a caterer?" His arm was mere centimeters from hers. Although they weren't touching, her body was tensed in anticipation.

"I do." She would have crossed her fingers at the lie if Jasper wasn't sitting so close. She did have *some* experience. Informal experience, but that was a start. Maybe she didn't technically know how to run a business, but she could cook. In that area, she was confident. And she'd decided back in Chicago that she would cling to that confidence.

"So really you moved back here to start your business." Jasper's finger finally made its way to her skin, traveling from her wrist slowly over her forearm and up toward her elbow, leaving a trail of tingles in its wake.

"Yep." Damn, she couldn't concentrate.

He turned, angling himself. His gaze flickered down to take in her lips, which she conveniently pursed for him.

What in the hell was she doing? She couldn't do *that*. Not with *him*. Could she? She supposed she was officially divorced now. Yes, she was a free agent. She could do anything—or, um, anyone—she wanted.

And maybe tonight, she wanted Jasper. Maybe she needed the connection with him because it had never felt so easy with anyone else. It wasn't like they hadn't slept together a million times already.

Confused, she threw back the final shot of tequila. Then she nodded to indicate his finger, which was still gently caressing her skin. "Jasper, what are you doing?"

His grin spread slowly but assuredly. "What do you think I'm doing?"

Even as the words left his mouth, she was moving closer to him. His eyes flickered down to take in her mouth, and she responded by biting her lip. She opened her mouth to say something seductive, something sexy. In a practiced move she used to perform all the time when she was younger, Carissa flipped her hair and placed her elbow up on the bar. Only, she missed the bar and nearly nose-dived into his lap, and she let out a very loud belch.

Embarrassed beyond belief, she shook her head.

Jasper grinned. "Yep, I think we may be done here for

the night." He pushed the mug with her remaining beer away from her.

"I'm not ready to leave." But even as the words left her mouth she let out a hiccup. When had she become buzzed?

"Last call," George bellowed out from the end of the bar to groans around the room.

Jasper nodded. "See, time for everyone to go. Not just you."

Carissa rose from the bar stool and almost toppled over. Whoa. Maybe she was a little more than merely buzzed. She had to grasp the edge of the sticky bar to keep from falling. "Gotta pay," she informed Jasper, who had already handed his credit card to George.

"I got it," he said.

"No!" she said defiantly.

"Consider it a welcome-back present."

"No," she repeated, trying to untangle the straps of her purse. "Gotta be independent. Can't rely on a man."

Jasper scribbled his signature on the check and turned to her. "You can't even get into your purse. Come on."

Suddenly, this seemed like a bad idea. She couldn't leave with Jasper, her ex-boyfriend. "Nope," she told him. "You hate me. Can't go with you."

"You have to go with me. I'm going to walk you to your aunt's house."

She swayed and tried to right herself, but Jasper had to reach out and steady her. "What will the peoples think?"

"I don't think 'the peoples' in this bar really care too much about anything except getting in one last drink order before George shuts down. Now, shall we?" He nodded toward the door.

Her head felt fuzzy. Thick and fuzzy. And she was very tired.

"Carissa Blackwell," Jasper said. "Get your hot butt out the door."

"You think my butt is hot?"

He made a show of looking around her back and then considering. "Yep. That is one fine behind. Now let me get a better view by walking to the door."

"Okay, but you're not the boss of me. I can get to the door by myself."

And with that she took two steps forward before tripping and ending up on the floor.

"Everything okay?" George asked, an amused expression visible, even under the depths of his beard.

"Yeah, I got this." Jasper turned to take in Carissa, who was currently in a pile on the floor laughing her head off. He sighed. He probably should have cut her off earlier.

After helping her up, Jasper waved good-night to George and the other patrons who were busy settling their bills. Then he ushered Carissa out the door and into the dimly lit gravel parking lot.

Even as he concentrated on getting her across the lot, he couldn't help but think about the night.

Carissa Blackwell was back in Bayside. Carissa Blackwell was divorced. Carissa Blackwell was incredibly drunk.

He didn't want to admit to himself that he'd been flirting with her. He'd looked into her eyes and gotten lost in old memories. Something he'd been adamant about *not* doing. Seeing her walk into The Rusty Keg had his insides all twisted up. The anger and hurt he'd felt all those years ago had bubbled up to the surface.

Then she'd admitted her husband cheated on her and something changed. Maybe because of the embarrassment that emanated from her when she told him. Perhaps it was the way her gaze flicked downward every time she said the word *divorce*.

Jasper wasn't entirely sure. All he knew was that the resentment took a back seat to caring.

Didn't take much to move closer and eye that tempting mouth. He shook his head. Everyone knew he was a big flirt. That's how he liked to communicate. And he hadn't seen Carissa in ten years, so they had a lot of communicating to catch up on. That's all.

They walked to the end of the parking lot. She was swaying and stumbling a little more than he would like to see. But cabs weren't abundant at this hour in Bayside, and he needed to get her home. She stopped in front of him, her long hair settling around her heart-shaped face.

"It was weird to see you tonight."

He didn't know what to say. That may be the truth, but still.

"But I'm glad I did," she continued. "You still make me feel tingly."

Tingly? Was that good or bad? "Really?"

"Yep," she said. "You were my best friend and my boyfriend. And you know what else? You were my first love."

Something softened inside him. "And you were mine."

"But now you hate me. Except for tonight when we're playing nice-nice."

He sighed long and loud, a decade's worth of angst spilling out. "I don't hate you."

"You're not happy with me," she said.

He shook his head. "No. Hey, it's your birthday though."

"Not anymore. Past midnight." She ran a hand down her side, highlighting her killer body. "Mmm-hmm." She licked her lips and those mysterious gray eyes met his and he lost all train of thought. He placed one hand at the back of her neck, pulling her toward him. With the other hand, he pushed a strand of hair behind her ear.

He shouldn't kiss her. He really, really shouldn't kiss her. And yet he was tilting his head.

Walk away, Dumont. But he couldn't get his feet to work. It was Carissa who finally broke the spell. She tilted her head up, lips pursed, eyes fluttering closed. Jasper met her halfway, pressing his lips to hers.

Instantly, he felt a spark. That feeling he only got with her. But it had been such a long time since he'd experienced it, he almost dropped to his knees.

Instead, he brought her closer and devoured her lips. She wound both arms around his neck, holding tight as she met his lips with equal desire.

The sound of a car starting snapped him out of the moment. "Damn," he said, looking around the parking lot, hoping whoever just got in their car hadn't seen anything.

When he turned back to her, he saw that her lips were swollen and her eyes hazy. He wanted to kiss her again right there and then.

"That didn't feel like hate to me," she said, her voice husky and appealing.

"Carissa…" he began.

"I broke up with you."

"I remember," he said.

She scrunched up her nose. "That was mean."

"Little bit," he admitted, and took a breath. "Why did you break up with me?"

"I can't tell you."

Amused by her, or maybe by the whole situation, he grinned. "Oh yeah? Why not?"

"Because there are three of you and um, uh, I'm dizzy."

Oh crap. He directed her to a tree stump on the road that

would lead back to town. "Do you need water?" he asked. "I can go back to the bar and grab a bottle."

She was taking long, deep breaths, focusing on the ground. She held a hand out. "No, just give me a minute."

He gave her ten. Once she appeared to get herself under control, she met his eyes. If he had any doubt about her being drunk, it was cleared up when she tried to stand and wavered. Decision made, Jasper put her arm around his shoulders and anchored her with an arm around her waist. Then they started walking slowly back to town.

"Where are we going?" she asked.

"To my place. It's closer," he said before she could argue.

"In Chicago, we can call cabs and Uber."

"Yeah, well, you're not in Chicago anymore."

"Nope." She looked up at him. "I'm here in Bayside, with you." Then she tapped a finger to the tip of his nose. "Boop."

Despite everything else, he laughed. "Okay, Boopy, let's keep walking. Maybe we can get to my condo by sunrise."

In the end it didn't take that long. Although it felt pretty onerous when Carissa launched into a rendition of her favorite Lady Gaga song, followed by some old-school Britney Spears. Carissa had many talents, but singing had never been one of them. He thought he heard some dogs wailing off in the distance and wondered if he would ever regain the hearing from the ear she sang/screamed in. In any case, he'd never been so happy to reach the center of town. Although if he was being honest, it was pretty nice to hear the sound of her voice again. Even her off-key voice.

Jasper simply pointed at the building that housed his condo across the street. "I'm going to take care of you for the night. I live there."

Carissa looked up. "I don't. Where's my house? Oh yeah, I lost it in the divorce."

He wasn't sure what she was babbling about but it didn't matter. They were in the homestretch. Just needed to cross the street.

And that's when Carissa let out a long, loud yawn and slumped against him. She was out.

"You are lucky you're not going to remember this because it would really piss you off." With that, he repositioned her body, took a deep breath and flung her over his shoulder, caveman-style.

He put all of his effort into carrying her, concentrating so hard that he almost missed when she murmured, "I really missed you."

Almost.

Chapter Four

Bayside Blogger @BSBlogger

Spotted at the Rusty Keg last night: Carissa Blackwell & Jasper Dumont. Reconciliation? Mayhaps. A better question would be, where did they end the night?

There were three things that Carissa did not need to open her eyes to know. First, the sun was streaming through a window, making her feel like a vampire being burned at the end of the long, dark night.

Next, she was fully aware that she'd had too much to drink the night before. Her head was pounding and her mouth was dry and gritty. She'd definitely consumed one tequila shot too many.

But most importantly, even with her eyes held firmly shut, she knew without a doubt that she wasn't alone. Someone was watching her.

"Morning, sunshine." Jasper's cool, calm voice rang out with a touch of humor to it from across the room.

"Hmphhjmelskjk," she mumbled incoherently as a reply.

"I thought you might say something like that." The mattress shifted and the rocking motion did nothing to appease her headache. "I'm going to grab you a bottle of water and some aspirin."

"Thanks," she ground out even as she buried her head further in the pillow.

But once Jasper was gone, she did finally peek out from her childish hiding spot. The events of the night before came crashing back. The evening had started off innocently enough with a trip to the grocery store. Then she'd ended up at the Rusty Keg with Jasper, where it was possible she'd drunk all of the alcohol in the whole world.

She searched her fuzzy brain and tried to remember all the particulars, but the details were slow to return. She knew she'd talked to Jasper for hours. She'd told him about her divorce and wanting to start her business. Then they'd flirted and she'd fallen on her face on the dirty bar floor, and then they'd gone outside and...

Her eyes widened and she shook her head back and forth, which only served to exacerbate her already-throbbing head. "No, no, no," she said aloud. They'd kissed. No, worse, they'd made out like they were still teenagers in the damn parking lot.

What had she been thinking? Well, nothing, duh. Thanks to the tequila. And the small part of her brain not coerced by alcohol had succumbed to the power of Jasper's clever lips. He'd always been an amazing kisser. She touched a finger to her lips now and that's when she remembered she was in a bed.

Carissa looked around. She saw her jeans on the dresser on the other side of the room. She flew out of the bed. She still had her tank top and bra on, but other than that, she was in her underwear.

At least this is a pair of my sexiest underwear. She berated herself. That wasn't the point. The point was that—

"You." She pointed at Jasper as he came back through the door, carrying a tray. "I don't have any pants on."

He grinned, his eyes roaming down her body. "I can see that."

"You took my pants off. You…you…"

"U, v, w, x, y, z."

She stared at him, mouth hanging open. "This isn't the time for jokes. Did we…"

Tray still in hand, he leaned back against the doorjamb, an amused expression on his face. "Did we what?"

She pointed at the bed and then at him and then back to herself. "Did we sleep together?" she whispered.

His face fell. "You were pretty drunk, Carissa. Give me some credit."

Immediately, she felt like a fool. Of course, he'd never do something like that. "Ohmigod, Jasper. I'm sorry."

"It's okay," he said.

She wrapped her arms around herself, suddenly aware that she must look absolutely disgusting. She was sure her hair went beyond a messy bird's nest. It was probably a whole bird mansion.

"I bring peace offerings." He held the tray up. "You look like you need these." He handed over a couple of aspirin, a plate with two pieces of freshly buttered toast, and a glass of water. "You shouldn't take those on an empty stomach."

She sank back onto the bed. "You brought me home and took care of me?"

"I didn't do much. You were out, um, pretty fast." He said that comment strangely and it had her head tilting. Then he quickly followed up with, "I slept in the guest room."

Damn, why did he have to be so nice? His sudden kind-

ness—so different from the teenager she remembered—
made her feel…things. A blush crept into her cheeks, and
desperate to hide her reaction, she turned to take a moment and admire his place.

His king-size bed was certainly comfy, decorated with
a fluffy, light blue duvet cover and matching pillows. The
furniture was all wood, very masculine. But the room was
tidy and there were amazingly tall windows, almost the
entire height of the wall, that let in the light she'd been
cursing a few minutes ago. If her head wasn't throbbing
she would be loving all that natural light and the view of
the water beyond.

She could see through the open door into the living
space. It was an open concept with brick walls, except for
one, which housed floor-to-ceiling bookcases. She shifted
on the bed, craning her neck to take in the kitchen, too.
But all she could make out from this angle was a large
island.

Jasper chuckled. "I can give you a tour, you know."

Her face grew hot. "Sorry. I don't mean to be nosy.
Just curious."

"I understand." He pointed to his dresser where her
capri jeans were neatly folded; her shoes sat on the floor
nearby. He nodded toward the left. "Bathroom's over there.
Why don't you take a moment and then meet me in the
other room?"

It was only then that she noticed he was dressed in
workout clothes. "Please do not tell me you've been to the
gym." She jumped up. "What time is it?"

He chuckled again but also held his hands out in a sooth-
ing gesture. "Don't worry, it's still really early. I never
sleep late."

She tilted her head in consideration. That was different from high school, when she'd always wait until at least eleven to call him on the weekends.

"I have some exercise equipment in one of the spare bedrooms. Helps me clear my head."

One of the spare rooms? "Exactly how big is this place?"

He grinned. "Three bedrooms, two and a half baths, a nice loft over the living room, and killer views."

A large, most likely expensive, condo. Just like she'd had with her husband in Chicago. Although her condo with Preston had been done in all beige and neutral tones, looking more like the model home real estate agents showed prospective clients than someone's living quarters. Jasper's place, on the other hand, had more of an edgy, urban vibe. Plus, she kinda wanted to marry these amazing wood floors.

"I'll go make us some coffee."

With that, he left the room and Carissa quickly chomped down the toast and swallowed the aspirin. Then she jumped from the bed, grabbed her jeans off the dresser and ran into the bathroom. Of course, she stopped to admire his killer walk-in closet on the way. The bathroom was just as nice and tastefully done as the rest of the place. Double vanity, separate soaker tub, and a shower that looked like it had no less than a hundred showerheads.

She stopped gawking at everything and she was very proud to say that she did not give in to the temptation to go through his medicine cabinet. Instead, Carissa quickly dressed, splashed some water on her face, did her best job of brushing her teeth with her finger, and ran a comb through her hair. Not a massive improvement, but definitely better than a couple minutes ago.

The aroma of coffee reached her nose and she followed it out to the kitchen. And if she thought she coveted the wood floors or the orgasmic shower, that was nothing compared to his kitchen. New stainless steel appliances, a farmhouse sink, and a gorgeous island that looked to be made out of reclaimed wood on the bottom and marble counter on top. She ran her hands along the cool stone and tried to keep from drooling.

"You like?"

"It kind of makes my aunt's tiny kitchen seem like an anthill."

"Is that where you plan to start your business from?"

"Of course." As he handed her a mug of steaming hot coffee, it occurred to her that he didn't realize her full situation. Jasper had no way of knowing that she was broke and desperate.

"You should consider renting out a space for a year or so. That would give you some separation. Plus, it would be better for meeting with clients. I could show you some places, give you a couple recommendations."

She sipped the coffee. "I thought we called a truce only for last night."

He considered. "Showing you real estate would be business."

Oh. Not really the answer she'd wanted. Then again, what did she expect? He'd been kinder to her than she deserved.

She ran a hand through her hair. "This coffee's good."

"Thanks. It's from The Brewside. A coffeehouse in the town square," he finished, clearly realizing she wouldn't be familiar with the changes in Bayside.

She put the mug down on the counter. "No, thank you. For getting me here last night, the coffee, for picking my clothes up, the toast. You didn't have to do all of that."

"I would have done it for anyone."

Again, not the response she'd expected. The sides of her mouth turned down in a frown.

"I would have let you sleep longer," he said, "but I have to get to work shortly and I didn't want you to wake up in a strange environment."

She eyed the clock above the stove. "It's still really early."

"I like to get into the office early."

"Of course," she said, and pointed toward the door. "I'll just get out of your hair."

"No, Car, I didn't mean you had to leave. Stay as long as you want."

She shook her head. "I'm sure you don't want some hungover girl lolling around in your place."

"I've had plenty of girls, hungover and stone-cold sober, loll around here." He snapped his mouth shut.

Plenty of girls. She looked away. What did she think? Jasper hadn't been dating for the last ten years? He became some kind of monk or something? Look at him. He was probably fending off women left and right.

"That didn't come out right," he said sheepishly.

Carissa held up a hand. "It's fine, Jasp. Don't worry about it." He seemed uncomfortable still. "What? Is there something else?"

He eyed his coffee mug. "Just something that happened last night. You probably don't remember but we…"

"Kissed," she finished. And what a kiss it had been. But after his "plenty of women" comment, she decided to keep that to herself. "I do remember."

"I'm really sorry about that."

He was? Because despite everything else, she wasn't sure that she was sorry. In fact, she kind of liked it. "Why in the world would you be sorry?"

He ran a hand through his hair. "You were drunk, Carissa. I took advantage of you."

She let out a relieved breath. "Jasp, we've kissed each other a million times before."

"I know, but…" He trailed off and she wondered what he wanted to say. Finally, he said, "More coffee?"

She shook her head. When he turned and crossed to the opposite counter to refill his own mug, his phone vibrated, dancing across the surface of the island. She tried not to look but couldn't help it. It was too close. Close enough to see a text message from someone named Simone Graves.

Morning, cutie. Sorry I missed having drinks w/u last nite. I'll make up for it. Promise. This was punctuated by a kissy-face emoji.

Wasn't it a tad bit early for emojis of any kind? Carissa couldn't contain the sigh.

"What was that for?" Jasper asked from across the room.

"Uh, nothing. Just exhausted." She was being ridiculous. Of course Jasper had women texting him. Was he serious about this one? Did he have a girlfriend? She searched her hungover brain. Did she even ask him last night?

"I'll bet." He crossed to the pantry and reached for a new box of sweetener.

She crossed the room and studied his very large collection of books on the floor-to-ceiling bookcases. Two entire shelves were devoted to graphic novels. She tapped them with a finger and let out a small laugh.

Then she returned to the island just as his phone lit up again. Someone named Sherry popped up on the screen this time. Me, you, our usual time and place. Don't be late.

Our usual time and place? Carissa gnawed on her lip as she considered. Just how many girlfriends did he have? She blew an errant hair out of her face. None of her business. Jasper had always been a flirt. Apparently nothing had changed.

Suddenly she felt nauseous and it had nothing to do with the copious amount of alcohol she'd consumed the night before. She pushed her coffee mug away and when she did, she noticed one last text message from someone named Elle.

4 calls in 1 day. All-time record, Jasp. Be back in town later today. Promise.

Simone, Sherry, Elle. Who were all these women? More importantly, why was she experiencing a sinking feeling in her stomach?

Because no matter what, and in spite of everything they'd been through, she would always harbor a very soft spot for Jasper Dumont. Always.

Admitting that was the first step. Now she needed to refocus. Worrying about Jasper and his apparently very active love life was futile. She had more important things to think of now, like her business. Because the one thing she knew was that no matter what, she needed time right now to concentrate on this business venture. No way would she end up like her father, relying on someone else for money and security.

An image of her Chicago condo all packed up with Preston's name scribbled on the majority of the boxes flashed into her mind. She wouldn't do that again. No, she was going to put everything she had into this business and it was going to succeed. And she simply couldn't get bogged down by a drunken night with her ex-boyfriend, no matter how nice he was the morning after and how many pieces of toast he made her.

She pushed back from the counter abruptly. "I, uh, should really get going."

Surprise shone in his eyes, but he quickly added a playful, "Worried you'll be spotted leaving my place the morning after?"

"Not particularly. Besides, nothing happened between us."

A shadow passed over his face. "Right."

"Right," she repeated.

A long moment stretched between them. Neither moved, neither spoke. Finally, Carissa backed up toward the door. "Listen, Jasp, don't worry about that kiss. In fact, don't even think about it. It was nothing."

"Really?"

Was it just her or did his expression darken? Maybe it was the light from the windows. "Yes. Like you said last night. We called a truce. Just…pretend it never happened."

"That's really what you want?"

It had to be. She nodded enthusiastically. "Yes. Absolutely. Go about your life. Continue dating, or seeing, or spending time with, whoever you might be doing those things with." She coughed. Why was she rambling? "Seriously," she finished when he opened his mouth to speak. "We are just old friends now." She ran a hand through her hair before taking the final step to the door. "Thanks again for everything. I guess I'll see you around."

With that, she made a hasty retreat from his beautiful loft, acting very much like she was worried she would be spotted the morning after.

The morning after a night like last night was enough to have Jasper dragging. He hadn't been drunk, but taking care of a drunk ex-girlfriend whom he'd securely placed in the "I'm definitely never seeing this person again" folder had been a bit much.

He ran a hand through his hair and then quickly cursed himself for messing it up while he was at work. See, one day in town and Carissa was already messing with his hair, not to mention with his lonely night out to drink away his thoughts.

He straightened in the leather chair behind his large oak desk at the Dumont Incorporated headquarters. If he was being truthful with himself, he hadn't actually minded taking care of Carissa last night. And he definitely hadn't minded that kiss. But wasn't that the problem? He should mind it.

He was going to have to chalk it up to nostalgia. He didn't harbor feelings for her any longer. In fact, he was positive they could exist in the same town without any emotional strife to speak of.

Besides, even if he was interested, which he clearly wasn't, she'd just gotten divorced. Although what moron divorced an amazing woman like Carissa was beyond him. Even more preposterous was the idea that anyone would cheat on her. That fact still set his blood boiling.

At least she'd decided to come back home instead of staying in Chicago. And now she was going to start a business, too. Maybe he could throw some contacts her way. After all, he was forever being invited to one party or another.

Leaning onto his desk, he nodded. He could definitely help her out. Not because she was an ex-girlfriend, though. He'd help anyone out.

"Right," he said aloud for emphasis.

"Everything okay, Mr. Dumont?"

Jasper practically jumped out of his seat at the sound

of his assistant's voice. "Yes, everything's fine, Sherry. Didn't I ask you to call me Jasper? Mr. Dumont is my dad."

The young woman smiled. Jasper had taken a chance hiring Sherry. Straight out of college with little experience. But he knew her family and Sherry had needed a job desperately. Luckily, she'd turned out to be one of the hardest workers on his team.

"Sorry, Jasper," she said. "Now on to our usual time and place."

"My favorite date with my favorite person," he said, referring to their usual morning rundown of his schedule and events.

"Yeah, yeah, I bet you say that to all the girls. Your two o'clock meeting switched to three," she said, beginning to go through her usual morning checklist. "I scheduled your dentist appointment for next week. Don't look at me like that. Even millionaires need to go to the dentist." She grinned. "I sent out those contracts first thing. Oh, and your brother called. Twice," she said, her smile fading. "I hope Elle is coming back soon."

Apparently, Jasper wasn't the only one Cam pestered when his better half was away. "This afternoon." They high-fived. "Anything else?"

"Nope, that's about it. Will you be heading to The Brewside for your usual morning pick-me-up?"

"Yep, about to leave. I'll bring you back a…" He waited.

"You know, my boss pays me quite well. He doesn't always have to treat me to coffee."

"Let me buy you a drink or you're fired."

She rolled her eyes, completely unaffected by him. "Fine. I'd like a medium chai. And thank you." She walked toward the door but stopped and turned back to him before she walked out. "Oh, and um, you might want to check out the Bayside Blogger's column this morning. Okay, bye."

With that, Sherry flew out of the room, returning to her workstation on the other side of the wall. Jasper sighed but quickly pulled up the *Bayside Bugle*'s site, found the link to the blog and started reading.

Well, damn.

The headline on this morning's blog was Homecoming Queen Returns to Bayside & Jasper Dumont's Condo.

It went on to detail how Carissa had been "spotted" fleeing Jasper's place that morning. He hadn't seen anyone around. He wondered how Carissa would take this. It had been a couple of months since he'd been featured on the blog. Typically, he always accepted the Bayside Blogger's attention with humility. But in this case, he knew he was about to start receiving calls and texts from his mom, his dad, his brother, and the list would go on and on. In an attempt to stave off the unwanted attention and questions, he grabbed his wallet, left his phone and headed out toward the coffee shop.

He was taking a risk showing his face there. The Brewside Café was the center of the Bayside universe, where citizens young and old gathered to gossip. Still, when a man needed coffee, a man needed coffee.

Gathering his energy, he hustled out of the building that housed Dumont Incorporated and walked the three blocks to the coffeehouse, which was situated right in the center of the town square between a shoe store and a clothing boutique. The Brewside, along with all of the establishments in the square, was painted a bright white and accented with blue shutters. There were two large flowerpots flanking the entrance. The flowers had seen better days, Jasper thought. Not unexpected, given the hot and humid summer they'd had. But he knew Tony, the owner, would soon change out the wilted flowers for something more representative of fall.

Jasper typically stopped by the café every day. Sometimes more than once. It was cozy inside with its old wood floors, rustic feel and arched ceilings with exposed beams. Wooden barrels served as table bases, and Tony had put either old doors or sheets of glass on top. An antique brass cash register sat on the large bar area, across from a glass display case holding every pastry under the sun.

Ordinarily, Jasper would take his time perusing the goodies before he ordered his usual large coffee. But today, as soon as he pushed through the door, every patron in the joint turned in his direction. He couldn't help but spot several copies of the *Bayside Bugle* throughout the place. Not to mention all the laptops and iPads littering the tables. Yep, the Bayside Blogger had reached her target audience.

Why fight it, Jasper thought. He gave a wave and continued to the bar to order.

He handed over his money and his "frequent buyer" card to Tony, who wore an amused expression.

"You're famous again, my friend," Tony said.

"Hey, I thought I was always famous in Bayside," Jasper replied with mock indignation.

Tony chuckled. "I suppose you are." He leaned forward, lowering his voice. "Is it true? Is Carissa Blackwell really back in town?"

Jasper wasn't sure how to answer but luckily he was saved by the bell as the chimes dangling on the inside of the door marked the arrival of a new patron. He turned to see a showered and changed Carissa stroll into the place. She looked as if she'd spent the night before getting a restful eight hours of shut-eye. No easy feat given her long drive the day before and her even longer alcohol-fueled night with him.

"Let me guess," Tony said. "That's Carissa Blackwell. I've heard stories about her." Tony didn't grow up in Bayside. He'd moved to town when he'd married a local and started The Brewside. The marriage didn't last, but Tony was considered a son of Bayside as much as Jasper was. Anyone plying the town with that amount of caffeine and baked goods would be. "She's as pretty as I've been told."

"That she is," Jasper agreed.

Tony handed Jasper his coffee and went off to help Carissa. Jasper noticed that everyone in the place was doing that thing where they tried to seem like they weren't ogling Carissa, only it made it that much more obvious that they were all staring at her.

She made some small talk with Tony, who, by all appearances, was eating out of the palm of her hand. She'd always been a charmer.

Then she turned and met his gaze. She looked amazing. Her hair was fluffy, her face scrubbed free of makeup, her eyes alert and completely the opposite of what they should be considering how much she'd drunk the night before.

She walked toward him, the flowy pants she had on billowing around her legs. She had on another tight tank top. This one was a deep aquamarine color that accentuated everything about her: her eyes, her skin tone, her body.

"Hey, Jasp," she said casually.

"Hey back," he returned. He tried to keep his voice calm even though the sight of her took his breath away.

"Here's your bagel with extra cream cheese and double-shot cappuccino, Carissa." Tony handed over a bag and cup.

She thanked him, then turned back to Jasper. Her eyes were taking him in the way a person on a diet viewed a double-chocolate brownie. He couldn't say he minded. The most beautiful woman he ever saw gawking at him? All was right in the world. Although after a few moments, he did have to ask. "Excuse me?" he said.

She coughed quickly and jumped back. "Huh?"

He chuckled and stepped closer. "Not that I mind, but you happen to be staring at me."

"No, I'm not," she said faster than Tony had called out his coffee order.

He took another step toward her. "Darling, I hate to argue, but you most certainly were staring."

A little crease formed as she drew her eyes together and Jasper thought it was the cutest thing ever.

"Do you always wear a suit to work?"

Her voice came out quiet but breathy as hell. Jasper had to take a moment to collect himself. Hearing her like that did things to his insides that no amount of coffee could cause.

"No, sometimes I go a bit more casual. But I have a couple meetings lined up for today."

"Oh. Well, you look…nice."

He tilted his head for her to follow him away from the counter. They set up camp at one of the high tables off to the side of the space. "Just as I suspected. You were undressing me with your eyes."

The shocked look on her face was priceless. "I absolutely, categorically was not undressing you or anyone else with my eyes. Or any other part of my body," she added quickly.

"As someone who could teach a class on how to undress people with their eyes, trust me, I have your number. But what I don't get is why. You, more than anyone, know exactly what's under here."

She gasped and swatted at him. "Oh shut up. It's been a long time since I've seen you naked." She took a long sip of her strong coffee, her eyes drifting closed in contentment. When she opened them, a small smile played over her lips.

"Better?" he asked.

"So much better. This will definitely help get me

through grocery shopping and unpacking." She frowned when she caught sight of a newspaper on the table next to them. She pointed at it. "Then there's that."

"You read it?"

"My aunt Val, who is currently across the ocean in Mo-freaking-rocco, called me an hour ago. Apparently there's an online site for this blogger person, too."

Jasper nodded. "I told you last night. She has a blog, a column, Twitter, Instagram, Facebook, Snapchat, you name it."

"Oh goody." She removed the bagel from its bag and began smearing it with a large amount of cream cheese.

He'd always envied her metabolism. "I can't believe you can still eat like that."

"There's always a silver lining, isn't there." She leaned forward and whispered, "Got divorced but I can still scarf down some yummy carbs without doing too much damage."

He covered her hand with his. "Things are going to get better, Car."

Jasper didn't have to turn toward the rest of the coffeehouse to know that they were being watched. "Sorry," he said, pulling his hand away.

"I imagine that's going to end up on one of the Bayside Blogger's many social media channels?"

"Does it upset you?"

She broke off a piece of the bagel and popped it in her mouth. Chewing, she seemed thoughtful. "Not really. I don't particularly like that someone knew I was leaving your place this morning, but it's not the worst thing that's happened to me this year. Still, I'd prefer it if from now on my business stayed simply that. Mine."

He agreed and was about to say so when the door opened, the chimes gave out their welcoming jingle, and someone walked inside. "Well, looks like we've got bigger problems than the Bayside Blogger right now."

She cocked her head. "We do?"

"Hi, Mom," he called over Carissa's head.

Carissa coughed, spitting the piece of bagel out of her mouth. She quickly wiped her mouth and hands and bolted out of her seat.

"Jasper, my handsome son." Lilah Dumont knew how to make an entrance. She breezed past the other patrons, doing her best Queen Elizabeth wave. She nodded at Tony behind the bar, who immediately started whipping up whatever drink she usually ordered. Then she turned back to the room as if to say, "please, be seated."

Jasper kissed her cheek. "You're looking lovely this morning."

She pinched his cheek. "Aren't you sweet." Then she turned her gaze to Carissa. "Well, well, the rumors are true. Carissa Blackwell has come home. You're looking as beautiful as I remember."

They hugged and Carissa said, "Thank you, Mrs. Dumont. It's great to see you."

"And you. Tony," she called. "Can you bring my smoothie and yogurt over here? Thanks, hon." She made herself at home by sitting right in between Jasper and Carissa. "I hope your parents are well. No one's seen or heard from them for years."

"Ma, don't start badgering her with questions."

"Oh hush," Lilah said. "I've known Carissa her whole life. So it's not badgering. It's simply being nosy," she finished with a smile.

"It's okay in any case," Carissa said. "Actually, I'm staying at my aunt Val's cottage while she's off traveling the world."

Jasper noticed the smooth transition. Also, the avoidance of discussing her parents. Interesting. He wondered what Mr. and Mrs. Blackwell had been up to for the last decade.

The two women talked about Val and her world exploits for a while. Tony brought his mother's food and smoothie to their table.

"So what brought you back to town?" Lilah asked.

Carissa shifted uncomfortably in her chair. Jasper quickly answered, "Carissa is starting a catering business here in Bayside."

"Really?" Lilah asked, delight in her voice. "What a wonderful idea. The closest caterer is a couple towns over and not always the most reliable. Have you been working in the catering field since college?"

"Well, um, actually..."

She was cut off by Jessica Monrow, an old family friend of the Dumonts. "Sorry to interrupt, Lilah, but I wanted to tell you that Edward will be able to make it to the party tomorrow night after all."

"Oh good, that's great news. Actually..." She turned toward Carissa and then back to Jasper. "Jasper, darling, have you invited Carissa to tomorrow night's event?"

He'd actually forgotten all about it. "Um, no, not yet."

"Oh right, you've probably only just run into each other." She arched her brow with that look she used to give him back in high school whenever he would come in from a make-out session with Carissa and she would pretend not to know.

Great, so his mother had read the paper and was aware that Carissa had spent the night. He felt his cheeks redden.

"Well, invite her now. I'm off with Jess to shop for a new dress. Carissa, lovely to see you. I'll look forward to catching up more tomorrow night. Jasper, clean this up for me, will you," she indicated the trash.

With that, Lilah Dumont made her grand exit.

"Well then," Carissa said. "Same old Mrs. Dumont."

"Quite the same," Jasper agreed. He checked his watch. "I hate to leave you, too, but I really should be getting back to the office. But why don't you come to the party tomorrow night?"

She shifted in her seat again. "Oh, Jasp, I really shouldn't go to that."

"Why not?"

She looked around the coffeehouse. "I mean, I've only just gotten back and I have so much to do. Plus, seeing half the town all in one place..."

"Trust me, if you can walk in here with your head held high after a Bayside Blogger article, you can do anything in this town."

She smiled but it didn't reach her eyes. He felt for her. She'd been through so much.

"You know, even though I've taken over Dumont Incorporated, my parents still have all those connections."

Clearly intrigued, she leaned forward.

"And all of those connections have connections. And collectively all of these people throw parties and luncheons and host events." He moved closer. "Parties and luncheons and events that require a caterer in order to be successful."

He saw it almost instantly. That small spark in her eyes that said he'd piqued her interest.

"You're saying that I should come to your parents' party for contacts?"

A new idea formed. But he quickly decided to keep it to himself. Instead, he changed his tone, challenging her. "I'm saying you would be a fool not to. And if I were you, I'd make sure to get there early."

She deliberated, taking another sip of her coffee. Finally, she gave a firm head nod. "Fine, I'll go." A sexy little smile spread on her face. "If this Bayside Blogger is going to write about me anyway, I might as well give her something to write about." She winked at him.

Jasper gulped. Somehow he had a feeling that today's article was not the only one that would feature the two of them.

Chapter Five

I don't want to start rumors. *Snort* But everyone is abuzz with the news that Carissa Blackwell will be attending tonight's Dumont soiree. Is it too early to come up with their couple name? I'm thinking either Jarissa or Casper? Let me know on Twitter by using the hashtag #ShesBack.

Carissa stalked around her aunt's cottage, doing the same thing she'd been doing the entire day. Admonishing herself over her behavior with Jasper the other night, dreading going to the Dumont party tonight and clearly avoiding unpacking.

She was an idiot. She had no business getting that drunk the other night. She'd been back in town for a whopping thirty seconds before she doused herself in tequila and cheap beer. Not the best way to start off her twenty-ninth year.

She slumped down at the kitchen table. Okay, so it hadn't exactly gone down like that. Jasper had been there for her that night. He'd listened to her sob story. Well, the parts that she'd actually shared with him. Worrying her lip, she debated whether or not to reveal to Jasper the real reason she'd broken up with him all those years ago. On the one hand, it would feel good to get that off her chest. But Jasper seemed so…well-adjusted now. Why bring up old hurts?

Besides, he'd moved on if all those text messages from other women meant anything. He probably never even thought about their breakup.

Damn, he'd looked amazing in his suit the other morning. Now, that was a great way to start the day.

"Stop it," she said abruptly. She needed to get her head out of the clouds and out of Jasper's suit and back into reality. She was back in this town so she could make something of herself. So she could be a caterer. So she didn't have to rely on anyone but herself. And so far, "herself" wasn't doing her any favors.

She rose from the table with a renewed sense of purpose. Everything was going to change tonight. She would slip on one of the fancy dresses she'd brought from Chicago and head to the Dumont mansion. She would wine and dine with Bayside elite, making contacts for her business, and hopefully get a lead on one single event she could cater.

If it came to it, she would beg.

"You can do this," she said out loud.

With that, she headed back to her bedroom and looked through her clothing options for the night. She remembered the Dumont parties from her teenage years. The Dumonts always went all out. Their parties were the social events of the year.

Her parents had always been invited, of course. Even before she and Jasper dated and were simply friends, they used to slink around the outskirts of the party, snagging hors d'oeuvres and dancing to the music. When they got older, they used to also steal a glass of champagne or two.

The first time Jasper told her he loved her had been on the beach at the bottom of the Dumont property. They could hear the music lingering from the band set up on the patio. They had toasted, completely unappreciative of what had no doubt been incredibly expensive champagne. The water was lapping at their feet. He kissed her, then he stared into her eyes, pushed her hair behind her ear and said *I love you*.

She'd been so dazzled, so mesmerized by him, that she'd simply said the same words back to him before falling into his arms.

But those memories were from a million years ago. Things were different now and she wasn't attending this party as a moony-eyed, boy-crazy teenager. She needed to establish herself. "Purpose, purpose, purpose," she said to her reflection in the mirror. Once again, she eyed her dress options. Finally, she chose one of her favorites. It was a sparkly, strapless number in a pale baby blue that brought out her light eyes. The dress skimmed the middle of her thighs, making her long legs appear even longer, especially when she paired it with her favorite pair of sinful silver stilettos.

After she added a pair of long dangly earrings, she swept her thick blond hair up on top of her head, leaving a few strands down to frame her face.

She put time into applying her makeup so it appeared as natural as possible. Then she double-checked her appearance in the mirror. Satisfied, she grabbed her clutch purse and headed out the door.

When she arrived at the Dumont mansion, it was still relatively early. In fact, the party hadn't started yet. She might have taken Jasper's advice to arrive early a little too literally. She could see servants putting the finishing touches on decorations and placing chairs on the tiered patios, and she heard the band warming up on the stage that had been set up for them.

As she walked through the impressive foyer and out the French doors that led to the backyard, the sounds of the instruments faded away. She didn't notice the mounds of beautiful flowers or the fact that the sun was setting over the bay in tones of red, orange, pink and yellow. Everything melted away as Jasper, dressed in a tuxedo with black pants, white jacket and black tie, turned from admiring the water to spot her. She froze, her mouth going dry as she inhaled sharply. Damn, he could give Chris Pine, Ryan Reynolds, or any other Hollywood leading man, a run for his money.

A slow, sinfully sexy smile blossomed over his face, making her fight to keep her knees from going out. Then he walked toward her with that confident gait.

"Hello, gorgeous," he said, his gaze raking over her.

"Hello yourself. Don't you look dapper." She had to stop from reaching up and fiddling with his tie. Or better yet, slipping her fingers underneath that crisp white shirt...

"Apparently, this is the final Dumont soiree of the summer season. I had to break out all the stops. But my tux is nothing compared to this little number." He wiggled his finger at her dress.

"Oh, this old thing?" she said coyly as if she wore short sparkly dresses on a daily basis.

He took another step toward her, his eyes darkening to a deeper shade of blue. He opened his mouth but before he could say whatever was on his mind, Mrs. Dumont darted out of the house. Even in the stunning yellow designer gown, with tasteful diamonds twinkling from her earlobes, Carissa could tell she was agitated.

"Jasper," she yelled across the patio in a very un-Lilah-like manner. "Oh, hi, Carissa. Don't you look lovely. Jasper, have you seen your father?"

"What's wrong, Mom?"

"Our caterer had a family emergency and she had to leave. I have no idea what I am going to do now."

"What about Joanna? My parents' chef," he explained to Carissa.

"She's on maternity leave. I knew we should have hired a backup chef. I told your father. But does he listen to me?"

"Can you run to the store and get some snacks?"

Carissa and Mrs. Dumont turned to him at the same time and both shouted, "No!"

"Go to the store for five hundred people?" Mrs. Dumont said at the same time Carissa said, "That's completely impractical, Jasper."

Mrs. Dumont turned to her. "Exactly. Not to mention that people expect a certain culinary experience when they come here The menu has been set for weeks and the oysters arrived not long ago."

Guests were starting to arrive. Carissa noticed a congregation at one of the bars. "That's horrible," she said to Mrs. Dumont.

"I just can't believe this happened. I always have a plan A, B and C. I guess I've gotten lax in my retirement."

"I have an idea," Jasper said. "Why don't you fill in?" He turned his attention to Carissa.

Her? Fill in for someone who was no doubt a world-class chef with decades of experience? After all, this was a Dumont event, not some little dinner party she was throwing for friends.

"Jasp, you're nuts."

"And you're a caterer," he countered. Then he leaned in and whispered, "This could be your big chance."

"Do you think you could handle it?" Lilah asked, hope filling her eyes.

Carissa glanced around as even more people streamed onto the terrace. "I've never catered an event this big." She realized that didn't sound like the best review and quickly amended her statement. "I meant to say, I usually work at much more intimate affairs. I'm not exactly used to an entire kitchen staff."

"Mom does have some great people back there though. I'm sure they could help you with any questions or concerns."

She bit her lip. Carissa understood what Jasper was saying. Catering an entire Dumont party would go a long way to helping her start her business. Then again, if she messed up, her business was dead on arrival.

A man around her father's age, with similar features, walked past them. Carissa thought about her dad. How he always took the easy way out. He would go into business, only to be derailed when the going got tough. Instead of fighting his way through it, he'd bail.

Sometimes, he wouldn't even start. If a project seemed like it was going to take up too much time or be too hard, he would pass.

Even as a teenager, she knew his attitude was all wrong. She knew she never wanted to be like that.

With renewed determination and a confidence she didn't quite feel, she lifted her chin. "Mrs. Dumont, I can help."

It took a lot to impress Jasper, but Carissa had managed to do it.

He peeked in the kitchen and couldn't suppress a grin when he found her still wearing that wickedly seductive dress with all that luscious hair piled atop her head. Someone had lent her a pair of sneakers, but even without those tempting strappy heels, her legs still managed to look amazing. Her dress was partially covered by an apron and the steam from the various pots on the stove gave her skin a dewy look.

Anyone could tell she was in her element. As soon as his mom had let her take a look at the catering menus, she'd gone into a no-nonsense business mode. She'd reviewed the menus, spoken briefly with the staff, washed her hands and immediately dived into work. Before Jasper or his mom could even say thank you, the appetizers had begun to appear.

He snagged a mushroom bruschetta from the counter now and almost had to close his eyes as the succulent flavor took hold. The woman could cook.

He reached for another and got his hand smacked for his efforts.

"Jasper Dumont," Carissa said, pinning him with a stare. "Those are for the guests."

"I'm a guest," he countered.

She pointed at the door. "Out!"

"Yes, ma'am." He wanted to tell her that her bossiness was turning him on but didn't think that would go over well with her Gordon Ramsay persona. Instead, he slunk outside, but not before quickly grabbing a carrot stick from one of the crudités platters. He retreated from the kitchen to the sound of Carissa's swearing.

The party was in full swing. Like most of his parents' events, it felt like the entire town had come out. His mother did usually invite everyone. Plus, there were plenty of colleagues, business associates and future business prospects. Jasper worked the party for a while, making small talk and promising follow-up emails and meetings. Then he skirted a table of desserts to avoid a woman he'd dated for a few weeks and firmly broken up with, but who didn't want to accept that. He spotted Simone in the crowd but was stopped by Aly, an incredibly intelligent brunette he'd spent an amazing ski weekend with in Aspen last year.

"Hey, Jasp," she cooed, happiness radiating out of her pores.

He tapped the large rock on her ring finger and grinned. "I hear congrats are in order."

She beamed. "Sorry you didn't snap me up when you had the chance?" she teased.

He put on his best mock-sad face. "I will forever regret it."

"I'll just bet." She laughed and wagged her finger at him. "I'm telling you, one of these days you're going to meet a woman who will bring you to your knees."

"Doubtful. Now that you're taken," he quickly added. He enjoyed hearing her laugh as she walked away to join her fiancé.

He chatted with his father, making plans for a round of golf in the following week. His dad wasted no time getting into full retirement mode. After seeing his dad work in some regard almost every day of his life, this change in behavior was a shock to Jasper. He had been sure he'd have to drag his father away from the office kicking and screaming. Still, his dad did manage to get in the usual fatherly concerns.

"Heard about the deal with Morris. Well done."

"Thanks, Dad."

"Now, remember, you can't just jump into that project with your usual gusto. Morris requires finessing."

"I know, Dad."

"You don't want to make one of your usual mistakes. That's all I'm saying."

Jasper held in a sigh, all of the positive vibes he'd been experiencing quickly draining out of his body. When was he going to be good enough? Even at his age, his dad could make him feel like that second son all over again. The kid that was not meant to take over the company. The one who couldn't possibly have the ideas and drive to run Dumont Incorporated.

"What are you doing with the waterfront property on Oak Avenue?" his dad asked.

Jasper shrugged. "Haven't decided yet."

"You know what I think."

Of course he did. His dad, as well as other members of the board, was intent to see him make a deal with the city over a prime piece of real estate. Jasper wasn't so sure that was a great idea. But this wasn't the time or place to get into that same old argument.

"Let's talk about that next week when we golf."

With that, Jasper made his way across the patio and took a moment for himself. He'd always loved his parents' house and particularly the expansive grounds. The back side of the house faced the bay with an abundance of French doors and windows to allow in the light and the stunning view. A large patio opened to a terrace, which cascaded down into more terraces—a scalloped effect that made for an amazing party setup. Guests could mingle in a variety of areas. Or they could chat around the large swimming pool or take a walk through his mother's gardens and end up at the tennis courts.

Naturally, his mother had several bars set up throughout the backyard, even though the drink of choice at a Dumont party tended to be the champagne passed on trays by waiters wearing white gloves. A little much in Jasper's opinion, but he did love that his mother never changed. She continued to throw these lavish parties with an overabundance of colorful flowers, mountains of food and the occasional fireworks display. In fact, he wondered if there would be one tonight.

On the main terrace he met up with his mother and brother, who were busy sampling some of Carissa's appetizers.

"How'd she do?" he asked his mother, referring to Carissa.

"I'm impressed. I'm happy. The guests are satisfied. And I want her to make whatever this is every single day for the rest of my life," Lilah said, acknowledging a cracker with some sort of pâté spread on it. "Thank God she returned to Bayside. I don't know what we would have done."

"I'm sure you would have figured something out," his brother Cam said around a mouthful of shrimp.

"Ohmigod, have you tried this?"

Jasper turned to see Cam's girlfriend, Elle Owens, and her best friend, Riley Hudson, strolling toward them.

"That's what I just said," his mother agreed.

Cam immediately snaked his arm around Elle, pulling her close to his side. Jasper was bemused to see big bad Cameron Dumont turn to goo every time little Ellie Owens was in his presence. The way Cam was lovingly watching her now, Jasper had a feeling it wouldn't be long until Elle was a permanent part of the Dumont family. Personally, he was thrilled at the prospect of a sister-in-law as amazing as Elle.

"Everyone's raving about the food," Riley added.

They really were, Jasper thought. He'd overheard his mother say that Carissa had mostly stuck to the menu but she did add a few twists of her own. Apparently those twists had everyone's taste buds singing her praises.

While Elle, Cam and his mom talked more appetizers, Jasper nodded at Riley. "Hey Ri, how's it going in the newspaper business?"

"No complaints. Did you read my latest column?"

"Would I ever miss a soon-to-be-Pulitzer-Prize-winning article on the importance of taking a proper selfie?" He winked at her and Riley laughed. She currently wrote for the *Bayside Bugle* in the Style & Entertainment section. Riley kept the town up to date on all the latest fashion trends, celebrity canoodlings, best restaurants in the area and all things related to the Real Housewives.

He sidled up to her. "I know I've asked before…"

"Jasperrrrr," she moaned. Elle and Cam tuned in.

"Come on, tell me. Who's the Bayside Blogger? I know you know."

Riley rolled her eyes. "You know I don't know. Just because I work at the *Bugle* does not mean that I know that one closely guarded secret. Only our editor, the workaholic Sawyer Wallace, knows that info. And he's not budging. Not even after what she wrote about me last week."

Elle scrunched up her nose. "That was kind of harsh. Everyone has a bad date from time to time."

"Exactly," Riley said. "There was no need to out me like that. Just because I spilled red wine on the poor guy."

"And had toilet paper attached to your shoe after you went to the bathroom," Cam said, trying to suppress a smile.

"And got sick in the parking lot," Jasper added, unable to control his grin.

"Hey." Riley poked him in the chest with her index finger. "That was not my fault. And I wasn't drunk. It was the clams. I'm telling you. Just wait until I have to do a review of that restaurant. Karma's a bitch."

"So is the Bayside Blogger," Elle put in. "I wish Sawyer was here. We could tie him up and force him to reveal her identity."

"Sawyer Wallace is not at my end-of-summer party?"

Mrs. Dumont looked quite offended. "He was invited, of course."

"He's working. Finishing up the weekend edition," Riley explained. "But he said he would be here a little later."

Jasper's mom gave a firm head nod. "Good. After all, Dumont Incorporated does enough advertising to keep that paper afloat." As she strolled away, Carissa emerged from the house. The apron and sneakers were gone, but she was still flushed from her exertion in the kitchen. When she reached the center of the terrace, people began to clap and his mother engulfed her in a big hug. As they chatted, with his mother clearly imparting her pleasure, Jasper was helpless to do anything but watch Carissa. Okay, maybe blatantly stare was a more apt description.

"Careful," Cam whispered in his ear low enough that neither Elle nor Riley could hear.

"What?" Jasper asked.

"Come on. If you were ogling her any harder your eyes would pop out."

Jasper took a swig of his champagne. "Hey, it's not my fault that a beautiful woman is standing right over there. Any man not staring at her is either dumb or blind."

Cam took a moment to look him over. Jasper almost started squirming under the scrutiny. Finally, Cam said, "You know what I mean. Just be careful."

"Careful with what?" Elle asked, sauntering up to them. Her hand found Cam's, and completely in sync, their fingers intertwined.

"Please don't tell me I made the firecracker shrimp too spicy. I really try to find a good balance." Carissa had appeared next to them.

Jasper couldn't help but notice Cam's smile fade. He did, however, compliment Carissa on her cooking. "It's all amazing and the shrimp were fantastic."

She smiled, an air of relief taking over. "Thanks. But if I had a kitchen like that and a staff of that many sous chefs, trust me, I'd never stop cooking. Good to see you again, Cam. I don't remember the last time I saw you without a full beard."

His brother was one of those kids who'd been able to grow facial hair earlier than most. In both high school and college, he'd donned a whole lumberjack appearance that had intimidated most people. Jasper would have laughed at Carissa's comment but he saw the way Cam was eyeing her.

"Welcome back," Cam said through gritted teeth. "Seems like just yesterday that you broke up with Jasper and left Bayside forever."

"Cam," Elle said in a very low, warning tone. "Welcome home, Carissa. Here you go." She offered a champagne flute, which Carissa accepted very tentatively. Despite the kind gesture, Jasper did notice a certain standoffishness with Elle, too.

Interesting, he thought. Carissa, Elle, Riley and he had all been in the same class in high school. He didn't remember any bad blood between the girls. Nor did he remember Elle and Carissa really being friends, either. Elle had been the smartest person in their class but her chief of police father had been really strict so Elle didn't tend to show up at the many parties he and Carissa went to. Riley, on the other hand, had been friends with literally everyone. Still was. She proudly held the title of social butterfly of Bayside.

Carissa took a deep breath, presumably centering herself. "Ellie…Elle—oh," she said, looking like she was putting something together. She shook her head. "Ellie, you look absolutely stunning. I'd heard that you'd moved to Italy." She gestured between Elle and Cam. "But it looks like you may have found a reason to come back."

Elle blushed. "Well, this burly man was not the reason I got on that flight home. But I'm certainly glad that he turned out to be my welcoming committee."

Carissa smiled and turned to Riley. "Ri, it's so good to see you."

Riley offered a hug. "You, too. Even though you never accepted my friend request on Facebook." She waved an accusatory finger but was smiling as she did so. "What's up with that?"

"Sorry. I'm not really on Facebook much, to be honest. Or any social media really. I just started that Facebook page because my husband wanted me to."

At the word *husband*, everyone seemed to freeze.

"Er, ex-husband, I mean." Carissa cast her eyes down.

Jasper wanted to jump in, save the day. But Elle and Riley exchanged a glance and quickly changed the subject. Before he realized what had happened the three of them were thick as thieves and had headed off to the dance floor. He wouldn't have minded joining them, but his mother returned.

"She is a beauty," his mother commented as she settled next to him.

He couldn't agree more. He didn't have to glance in her direction to feel that his mother was pinning him with a hard stare. "Watch yourself, Jasper," she said in a serious tone.

He let out a long exhale. First Cam and now his mom. His family was acting like he was some innocent little girl with a red cape and basket and Carissa was the big bad wolf waiting to pounce. "You have nothing to worry about, Mom."

"Don't I? My youngest child is staring at someone like she's the only woman on the planet."

"She's gorgeous. You said so yourself."

"She's also the only woman who's ever broken your heart." At the sharp edge in her voice, he finally met her stare. "Remember, I was the one who saw you after she hightailed it out of Bayside without stopping to look back."

"She just saved your party."

"And I'm grateful for that. I plan on recommending her to anyone who will listen." She grabbed a flute of champagne from a passing waiter, took a delicate sip, then returned her attention to him. "Don't think that I don't like Carissa. That's not what this is about."

"Then, what's it about? That she broke up with me when she was eighteen years old?"

Her lips quirked. "Well, no mother likes when someone dumps their child. But no, that's not it. I like her. But I love you. You know what comes with loving a person?" He shrugged. "Worrying about them."

He draped his arm around her shoulder. "You don't have to worry about me. I'm a big boy."

She nodded in Carissa's direction. "Not where she's concerned. I just don't want to see you get hurt again."

Neither did he.

He'd always had an open, honest relationship with his mom, so Jasper didn't have any trouble being truthful now. "I don't know that I could ever forget the hurt she caused me. I don't know that I want to." He paused, collecting himself. "Doesn't mean I can't be friendly. Or admire that dress." He wiggled his eyebrows.

Lilah batted his arm. "Behave."

"Never." He pointed out Simone Graves. "See that woman over there? We're going out soon. In fact, I'm going to go check in with her now." He started to walk away but turned back. "You really have nothing to worry about." With that, he continued toward Simone.

But if Jasper had turned back again, he would have seen

his mother shaking her head, a knowing and doubtful expression on her face.

Simone seemed ecstatic when Jasper made his way to her. He produced a champagne flute from behind his back.

"Jasper Dumont, aren't you sweet." She stepped closer and whispered in his ear. "I'm excited for our date."

"Me, too," he replied, but a movement to his right caught his eye. The dance floor was getting busy and Carissa had just thrown her head back and laughed, her husky voice floating over the other noises of the party and hitting him right in the gut.

"Don't you think?" Simone was asking.

What? "Oh yeah, right."

Jasper and Simone made more small talk. Ordinarily, Jasper loved nothing more than enjoying champagne and flirting with a beautiful woman at one of these parties. And Simone was fun, sweet and bubbly. Some of his favorite qualities in a woman. But tonight, he couldn't seem to keep his gaze from the dance floor.

He noticed Robbie Hartwell, a guy he employed at Dumont Incorporated, move toward Carissa. He sucked in a breath. Robbie was a great addition to a poker game, but he was a player away from the card table, as well.

"Why are you frowning?" Simone asked, oblivious to his inner thoughts.

"Uh…because you're already out of champagne," he covered smoothly. "Would you like another?"

"I think I'm okay. There's an early-morning Zumba class I want to hit at the gym tomorrow."

"Uh-huh," Jasper said absentmindedly as he continued to eye the dance floor. He let out a breath when he saw Carissa shake her head and Robbie walk away.

He continued talking to Simone.

"Right now, I teach dance to little kids part-time. But I'd love to open my own studio."

Jasper tried to concentrate on Simone's words, but it was hard when Carissa was right across the patio shimmying around the dance floor with Elle and Riley. Her short sparkly dress hugged every curve and seemed to be getting even snugger in the late-summer humidity. His mouth went dry.

"So what is it you do?" Jasper asked.

"Um, I just told you."

He snapped to attention and took in Simone's confused face. "Uh, sorry. It's been a long week." He couldn't stop himself from glancing toward the dance floor one last time.

"Hey, are you looking at…" Simone trailed off as she also took in the dance floor. "Is that Carissa Blackwell?" She peered closer.

"Do you know her?"

"Not really. I was a freshman when you guys were seniors. Every girl in my class wanted to be her. She was the captain of the cheerleading squad, she lived in that amazing house by the water and she was so, so beautiful."

Still is. Jasper shook his head and tried to focus.

"There was this rumor that an agent had spotted her at the mall and wanted to take her back to Hollywood to be in movies. And that's why she and her parents disappeared from Bayside."

Jasper chuckled. He wondered what Carissa would think about that. "Never happened to my knowledge, and I knew her pretty well."

Simone turned back to him. "Of course. I'm an idiot. You guys dated. Hey, didn't she, like, break up with you after graduation? There was another rumor that she was into a college guy."

"Not to my knowledge," he repeated. "I mean, we did

break up. It's great to see her again," he added as flippantly as he could manage.

Simone ran a hand over his chest and leaned in to whisper in his ear. "And it will be more than great to see you without all these people around."

He couldn't help it. He slid one last glance in Carissa's direction. *Be careful.* Both his mother and his brother had uttered those ominous words. But there was nothing to be careful over. Carissa was back in town. That didn't mean anything. He'd helped her the other night when she'd been drunk. He would have done that for anyone.

And the kiss they'd shared? Ordinarily, Jasper wasn't one for kissing more than one woman at a time. He liked to date. Some even called him a perpetual dater. He didn't mind that, because whoever had his attention at the time was the only one who had it. He had a firm rule of one woman at a time. Even if he only dated a woman for two weeks, he was completely monogamous for those two weeks.

True, he hadn't gone out with Simone yet, so kissing Carissa the other night didn't break his rule. Still, he'd prefer to keep things as uncomplicated as possible. That's why he'd have to rule their kiss the other night as nothing more than a little slip into the past.

Besides, Carissa had been adamant about the kiss meaning nothing. What had she said before she made her quick escape that morning? Something about how he should continue with his life. Couldn't get clearer than that in Jasper's opinion.

He took in Simone's big chocolate eyes, waiting for his answer. He would go out with Simone and that would show everyone that he was no longer stuck on Carissa Blackwell.

"Sounds perfect," he said, and gave her a quick peck on the cheek.

As he pulled Simone into his arms for a dance, though, he couldn't help but notice that he wasn't alone in staring. Across the dance floor, Carissa was watching him, as well.

Chapter Six

What a night! Who else was impressed by a stunning Carissa Blackwell saving the party by filling in for the runaway
caterer? Not everyone, apparently. My sources tell me that
Jasper's big brother is anything but happy to see Carissa
back in Bayside. Will Cam's long memory ruin any chances
for a Jasper-Carissa reunion? We'll have to wait and see...

Carissa made her way to The Brewside the morning after
the party. She'd walked over from her aunt's cottage, excited to continue her high from the night before. But as
she neared the coffeehouse, her anxiety level started rising. Now she stood right outside the door, taking a moment
before she entered.

While they'd been dancing together the night before,
Elle and Riley had invited her to meet up in the morning
to dissect the night's events. Well, Riley had invited her
anyway. Carissa hadn't missed the look Elle had slid in Riley's direction when she'd extended the offer.

Not that Carissa could blame her. Carissa had never been
a mean girl. But with some age and perspective, she had

to admit that she'd hung out with a couple of mean girls. And those mean girls had given their best to Elle back in high school. Just because Carissa hadn't been the one doling out the insults and snickering behind Elle's back, she'd known it was going on. And then, of course, there was that video they'd made of her that had completely humiliated the poor girl and maybe even driven her from town altogether.

Carissa stepped back from the door. What was she thinking? She couldn't go in there and pretend that video had never been made. She needed to hightail it back to the cottage. Mind made up, she took another step backward and ran directly into someone.

"Hey, girl, great timing." Despite how late the party went last night and how early it was now, Riley looked fresh and comfortable in linen pants and a flowy tank top. "Elle just texted me. She'll be here in five minutes."

"Listen, Ri, I really don't think I should..." But she couldn't finish her thought because Riley had linked arms with her and was pulling her inside the coffeehouse. Her unease abated slightly when the enticing aroma of ground coffee beans and freshly baked goodies made its way to her nose.

"I'm dying for coffee. What can I get you?" Riley asked.

"What? Oh, you don't have to do that."

"No problem. Think of it as your welcome-home coffee."

Carissa ran a hand through her hair. "Um, thanks, but I'm not sure everyone is as excited I'm back as you."

Riley simply waved a hand through the air as if Carissa was speaking nonsense. "Go grab us a table."

Resigned, Carissa did as instructed, and soon she was joined by Riley, two lattes and a bundle of nerves in her stomach. The best thing to do was to lay it out on the table and apologize for the past. But when Elle walked through the door, her confidence faltered.

Elle waved at them and then headed for the counter, placing her order.

"Are you okay?" Riley asked. "You seem tense."

Carissa didn't have time to answer.

"I need caffeine and carbs," Elle announced as she slunk down in her chair with her coffee and a large bag. She pulled half a dozen bagels out of the bag. "I bought a variety. I knew you would go for the blueberry bagel. You are so predictable, Riley Hudson."

Riley smiled as she immediately started applying strawberry cream cheese. "Sorry if you wanted the blueberry, Carissa, but it's mine. All mine!"

Carissa ignored the amazing-smelling bagels and took a deep breath. "Elle, I'm really, really sorry if I was a bitch to you." Both Elle and Riley froze. "In high school, I mean."

Riley still had half a bagel in one hand and a knife loaded with cream cheese in the other. Elle was holding two sugar packets over her coffee. Neither of them had blinked since she started rambling.

"Er," Elle finally mumbled in confusion.

"I know, this is completely random. But I sort of sensed last night… I was grateful for the two of you dancing with me and inviting me to breakfast this morning. I suspect you didn't really want me to be here, though. I mean, it makes perfect sense for you to give me the cold shoulder."

"Huh?" Riley asked.

Carissa couldn't stop herself. She wasn't the best apologizer. "To be honest, I knew you had a crush on Jasper back in high school, Elle. I think everyone did. I wasn't threatened by it. And I don't really get jealous. Not over stuff like that. I mean, I just felt really secure in my relationship with him. You know? Oh God, does that make me snotty?"

"You need to breathe, girl," Riley said.

"I want you to know that I had nothing to do with that video my friends made of you."

Something passed over Elle's face. She lowered her eyes and pursed her lips. Then she finished fixing her coffee, took a sip and locked eyes with Carissa.

"I know you didn't have anything to do with that video."

Back in high school, Elle had been as shy as she was smart. She'd worked hard to become the valedictorian. And, yes, she'd also had a hopeless and passionate crush on Jasper. Toward the end of senior year, Carissa's friends had invited Elle to a sleepover. They'd spiked her drink and taped her professing her love for Jasper. They didn't leave it there, though. They played it during senior prom in front of everyone. Elle was humiliated and had her valedictorian status stripped from her after she'd been shown drinking.

Carissa heard that Elle went to college and then off to Florence, Italy. Gone from Bayside for a decade because she felt she'd embarrassed her father, who had lost his election to become county sheriff due to the scandal. Carissa knew all about leaving Bayside and embarrassments behind. But while she'd left willingly, Elle had not.

Elle took a deep breath. "Your friends were mean, Carissa. But you never were. At least, not to me. I mean, we didn't speak all that much. If I was weird or cold or distant last night it's because I was the one who professed my love for *your* boyfriend. I should be apologizing to you. Not the other way around."

Carissa couldn't believe what she was hearing. "No, no, no, I really am sorry."

"So am I," Elle countered.

Riley snickered. "How about we call it a truce and say you're both sorry? We're all adults now. Can we eat these bagels and gossip yet or what?"

All three of them laughed. With the past settled, they enjoyed their breakfast and chatted about the party the night before. Riley and Elle filled Carissa in on the new faces in town and refreshed her memory on some of the people from high school.

When their bagels were consumed, Riley leaned forward. "Well, I'm glad the past is in the past and we can all move forward as friends."

"I do have to ask, though. Is that the reason why Cam was giving me the cold shoulder and a bunch of not-so-friendly stares last night?"

Elle bit her lip. "I'm sorry he was being that way. Unfortunately, I think it's only part of the reason."

Carissa waited for a moment before she realized. Idiot. "And the other part would be that I dumped Jasper after graduation."

Elle nodded but Riley snorted. "Yeah, the dumping sucked. But I think it's also the fact that you never contacted him again. Like, not ever. In fact, you never contacted anyone from Bayside after you left," Riley finished. "What was up with that?"

Carissa could feel her cheeks heating up. "I wanted a clean break." She sat back in her chair and took a long, deep breath. Then she met her friends' eyes again. "The day that Jasper and I broke up, well, I said some things to him that I'm not proud of. I told him he had no ambition, no drive. I didn't want to be with someone without any goals."

Little did Jasper, or anyone else for that matter, know that she'd found out that very morning that her parents had run out of money. Her father had blown through her mother's very large trust fund. Since he was always in and out of jobs, he had no real experience to fall back on. Parties and socializing had been more important to him than ensuring that his wife and daughter were taken care of.

She'd been eighteen years old and the proverbial rug

had been yanked out from under her. The fact that her relationship with her father had always been on the rocky side didn't help matters. She might react differently today, but back then she'd been embarrassed. And angry. And scared.

Carissa had to spend the summer figuring out how to pay for college, which she had done with the help of her aunt Val. But those four years at Northwestern had been tough. She'd studied her butt off while holding down three different jobs.

Fearing that all their important friends in Bayside would find out that they were now poor as church mice, her parents had moved to New England where her mother had taken job after job to make ends meet. When Carissa found out that her dad still wasn't pulling his weight, she'd been furious.

Jasper reminded her of her father. They were both so handsome and the life of every party. All charm and no ambition. At least, that's how he'd been in high school. Spent his parents' money and partied with his friends. Not a care in the world. Not a mention of a future. He slept until noon on weekends and never really cared about college or anything beyond that.

She remembered walking to meet Jasper the day she'd broken it off with him. All she could think about was if Jasper was so content to breeze through life at that point, what would he be like when they became adults? Would he repeat her father's behavior? Would she then go through another period of embarrassment? Of anger? Of fear?

Carissa shook her head and continued. "Although what I said to Jasper back then doesn't seem to have stopped him. He's doing amazingly well now. Even with everything I said to him that day."

"Maybe he's doing so well *because* of everything you said to him," Elle said.

She cocked her head to the side. "What do you mean?"

Elle and Riley exchanged a look.

"Come on, spill," Carissa said.

"Cam told me that after you left Bayside and after Jasper got over his initial shock at the breakup, he turned his life around."

"Well, that's good."

"It is, in the end."

Carissa couldn't miss another look between Elle and Riley. "There's more."

Elle nodded. "He threw himself into studying. He took job after job to learn as much as possible about business from the ground up."

Riley sat forward. "He became…obsessed."

In Carissa's experience, the word *obsessed* was generally not a good thing. It was usually a drastic reaction to something.

To hear that her words caused Jasper to alter his life—even if his life ended up better because of it—made a pit form in the bottom of her stomach. Maybe she was more of a mean girl than she realized.

"Hey, don't worry about it." Riley shook her arm. "Jasper's right where he was meant to be. And so are you."

Carissa let out a tiny laugh. "Where's that exactly? Living in my eccentric aunt's cottage because I got a divorce?"

"Basically." Riley toasted her with her coffee. "You're with us and I think the three of us are going to be really good friends."

She hoped so because Carissa could certainly use friends. Not to mention, she could use money if she ever wanted to get out of her aunt's place.

"So now that we're all friends and sharing secrets," Elle began. "I have to ask. You're completely over Jasper?"

"Of course," Carissa said quickly. Maybe a bit too quickly. "I just got divorced like five minutes ago."

"That's not really an answer," Elle said.

"Besides," Carissa continued, "I saw Jasper with that redhead last night." And that had stung a little. She hated to admit it. Jasper was at liberty to date whoever he wanted. But at the same time, they had kissed the other night. When she saw him pull that pretty woman into his arms, she'd almost tripped on the dance floor. Wasn't that just silly?

"That's not an answer, either," Riley countered.

Carissa sighed. "Okay, then let me be clear. I do not have any romantic feelings for Jasper Dumont. Or anyone else, for that matter. I am here to start my catering company. I just need some business."

Just like that, the front door of The Brewside opened and in waltzed Jasper's mother. Once again, she didn't have to give her order. Tony had it ready for her in a minute. She scanned the room, saying hello and accepting compliments on last night's party. Finally, her gaze fell on Carissa, who had to wonder if she shared Cam's judgment of her. But her lips quirked, turning into a beautiful smile. A smile that definitely reached her eyes. Carissa's stomach settled.

"Carissa, I'm so glad to run into you here. Hello, Riley, Elle—darling." She gave a quick hug to Elle, who would more than likely be calling Lilah Dumont mother-in-law soon. "I was going to stop by your aunt's cottage."

"You were?" She couldn't keep the surprise out of her voice.

"I wanted to thank you again for saving the party last night."

Carissa smiled. "I don't know if I saved anything, but I'm glad I could help out."

"So am I." Relief washed over her face. "I also wanted to give you this." She handed over an envelope.

Curious, Carissa opened the flap and took a peek. It was a check made out to her, and the amount almost had her falling off her chair.

"I didn't know your catering company's name so I just made it out to you. I hope that's okay."

"It's fine. I don't actually have a name yet. But I wasn't expecting any payment."

Lilah waved a hand. "Nonsense. You did a job, completed a service. Of course you should be paid. You saved the day."

Carissa was about to protest again, even as she tightly clutched the check in her hand. But Riley piped up. "That's it. Why don't you call your company Save the Day Catering?"

Elle's eyes lit up at the name. "Great idea."

Carissa mulled it over. Save the day. And she really would love to save someone's day with her cooking. No one needed to know that starting this business would also be saving her. "You know, that's not bad. Save the Day. I like it."

"It's settled. A very productive morning," Mrs. Dumont said. "And I think I can add to it. Carissa, I'm hosting a ladies' tea and I would like you to cater it. It's on Wednesday, so short notice."

"Not as short as the five minutes she had last night," Elle said kindly.

"I think it was more like two minutes, actually," Mrs. Dumont said. "If you are willing, I'd like basic tea party food. Sandwiches, scones, tea cakes, that sort of thing. What do you say?"

Carissa was floored by the generous check first and now by the opportunity for more business. Mrs. Dumont's offer was more than she could have expected. What a great way to start her business.

"That would be amazing. Thank you so much. Why don't we set up a call for later this afternoon to go over the logistics?"

"Perfect," Lilah said.

Carissa was so busy reveling in her thoughts and good fortune that she'd tuned out of Elle and Mrs. Dumont's chitchat. Tuned out, that is, until she heard Elle ask what Jasper was up to today.

"He has a date with some new girl." She waved her hand in a flippant manner.

Riley rolled her eyes. "There's always some new girl. Good luck to this one, too." Mrs. Dumont laughed with Riley. But Elle reached over and patted Carissa's hand.

"It's fine," Carissa whispered so only Elle could hear. "I told you I'm not interested in him like that."

"I know." Elle squeezed her fingers. "But just in case you needed it."

What was that supposed to mean? Jasper was free to do whatever, or whomever, he wanted. She wished him well. If he wanted to spend an evening with that perky little redhead, then more power to him. Maybe they would really hit it off and get married. But she'd been down that road before. So good luck to them both.

In the meantime, she had a new purpose. She was starting a company and thanks to Mrs. Dumont, she already had her first assignment.

See, much more important things to think about than Jasper's love life. Not that she cared anyway. Not one little bit...

Jasper was at an amazing restaurant, enjoying a particularly good sauvignon blanc with a stunning woman. The food was great and the ambience was romantic. The perfect date.

Only, it wasn't, and not only because Jasper's mind was a million miles away from Simone and the Boat House.

Jasper sipped his wine and stifled a laugh as Simone regaled him with a story of her Zumba class as she simultaneously finished a third glass of wine. Deep down, he tried to figure out why he wasn't enjoying this night more. He'd been out with plenty of flirtatious women. Usually he loved hearing about their lives. But tonight, he just wasn't feeling this.

He'd had a nice Saturday. Spent some time with his brother, did a little bit of work, went to the gym. Plus, the party had been fun last night, he thought as Simone switched topics and started filling him in on the recent episode of her favorite reality show.

Carissa had seemed to enjoy herself last night. He wondered if she'd made any business contacts. Of course, she'd been in the kitchen for the first half of the night and then shimmying around the dance floor for the rest. She'd looked good out there. Reminded him of watching her cheer at football games in high school.

"Do you agree?" Simone asked, ripping him out of his thoughts.

"Uh, totally."

Simone scrunched up her nose. "You do?"

"Of course not," he said, completely confused. "I was messing with you."

Simone relaxed back against her chair. Jasper tried to clear his mind of Carissa and her dancing. Instead, he focused on the dessert menu. There was a seasonal favorite on the list, peach pie. His mouth watered at the thought.

The waiter came by and asked if they wanted dessert. Jasper opened his mouth but Simone beat him to it. "No, we're fine. Just the check please."

"Really?" he asked. "No dessert?"

Simone shook her head. "One night of dessert equals a month of gym time."

He couldn't help but think of Carissa and how she'd devoured her bagel and cream cheese the other morning. No way would she pass up dessert. But in the end, Jasper pushed his disappointment aside, especially since his mind had been wandering all night. All he could concentrate on was the image of the dress Carissa had been wearing at the party. How every time she moved on the dance floor it would inch just a tiny bit higher, revealing her long, toned legs.

The check came and Jasper reached for his wallet. After leaving the restaurant, he and Simone walked around the water hand in hand. Jasper realized he had been on this date many times over the years. Nice restaurant, pretty evening walk, and, if it was a good night, a return to his condo. But he was sure taking Simone home would not be a good idea this evening.

"And, of course, I don't see why people are down on reality shows. I'd love to be on one. Don't you think I'd be great on a reality show?" Simone didn't wait for an answer. "I mean, to be like the Kardashians. They're so amazing. And smart. People don't think they're smart, but come on. I mean, hello! What about their clothing lines?"

"I guess," Jasper added. He had no idea what she was talking about.

"Not to mention, they marry well. People can say whatever they want but I don't see a problem with a woman wanting to marry a rich man. Do I want to be poor?" She let out a little chuckle. "Um, of course not."

Red flag, red flag. If Jasper had been wearing a tie, this would have been the point when he loosened it.

"Not that I wanted to go out with you because you're

rich. Obviously, everyone knows you have money. You're a Dumont."

This conversation had gone south quickly. "Yes, I am."

"So," Simone said, turning to him and puckering her red lips.

"So," he countered lamely. Jasper repressed the urge to roll his neck. "It's getting late. We should probably get home."

She stepped closer. "What a great idea. I've been dying to see your place," she said boldly.

Ordinarily, a statement like this would have left him grinning and taking off for his condo at record speed. After all, the last woman he'd brought home had been...Carissa, he realized with a jolt.

"Actually, I was thinking I should drive you home. I'm sorry," he quickly added at her frown. "I have a really early morning tomorrow."

Simone crossed her arms over her chest. "Tomorrow is Sunday."

"Right, well, I have some work I need to catch up on and you said you have that exercise class."

She nodded slowly but didn't look at all convinced. Jasper couldn't blame her. "You know, Jasper, this has been a really great night. But I have to admit that I've had the feeling you'd rather be somewhere else. I mean, you didn't even think my story about the youngest Kardashian liking my tweet about lip gloss was interesting."

"I'm sorry, Carissa."

She let out a laugh, but the sound was harsh. "I suppose that's my answer."

"What?" he asked, confused.

"Jasper, you just called me Carissa."

He wanted to cover his face with his hands. He might not have enjoyed his date with Simone, but he was never,

ever disrespectful when it came to women. Calling her by the wrong name was unacceptable. He pulled her into a hug. "I'm really sorry about that, Simone."

"You know, the Bayside Blogger has been speculating about you two since Carissa got back to town last week. Even though I was younger, everyone in school knew how intense you guys were when you dated."

Intense? That was one way of looking at it.

"I'd wondered if you were interested in getting back together with her, but since you still wanted to go out…"

"Oh no. I don't want to get back together with Carissa and I'm sure she feels the same way about me."

Simone tilted her head. "Really? Because she kept staring at you last night at the party."

"Really?" Jasper asked quickly. Too quickly, if Simone's huff was any indication. He shrugged and tried to play off his comment. "Trust me, nothing's happening with us and nothing is going to happen. I guess I just called you by her name because this is where I saw her when she first returned to town. I hadn't seen her in over a decade." He squeezed her hand. "And I did want to go out with you."

"Really?"

"Yes, of course."

Her gaze drifted to the side as she considered. "Then, how about this. You take me home tonight. And maybe we can try another date next week?" She smiled, showing her dimple. One of the things that he'd been drawn to when he'd first talked to her. "I'd love to introduce you to my mom and sisters."

The red flag turned even redder. Meeting the family after one date? He didn't think so.

"I think we may want different things, Simone," he said honestly. "You're wonderful, but right now, I need to concentrate on my career. You should be with someone who can devote every waking hour to you."

This seemed to appease her, and they walked back to his car and Jasper held the door while she got in. Then they began driving away from the town toward Simone's place. She was renting an apartment not far from Carissa's aunt's cottage.

There he went, thinking about Carissa again. He tightened his hands around the steering wheel. Why couldn't he get her out of his mind? Wasn't it bad enough that she'd already ruined a perfectly good date?

Okay, maybe the date with Simone hadn't been the best of his life. If only he'd been more into reality television and the E! network. But she was still an attractive, fun, energetic, talkative female. Moreover, she was a female who had never ripped his heart out and fed it to him before disappearing from his life.

Jasper cursed under his breath. The first thing he was going to do after dropping Simone off was get a drink and put a concerted effort into not thinking about Carissa Blackwell.

When he reached Simone's place, he walked her to the door and gave her a quick hug. Before she inserted her key into the lock, she paused.

"If you change your mind about going out again, you know how to reach me."

"Absolutely."

At least she was being a good sport about the evening. From his obvious lack of attention to calling her the wrong name, a lot of women would have written him off immediately. In the end, he knew the two of them weren't a fit. And despite her offer, he knew she did, too.

Jasper hustled back to his car and began driving home… and continued to try and shake thoughts of Carissa from his head. Obviously, it wasn't her fault she was stuck in his head. Still, he was supposed to be over her. Isn't that what he kept telling everyone else?

He took a right, and as he went around a curve, he saw a black car on the side of the road. He slowed, and as he did, he watched a tall woman wearing jeans and a pink T-shirt yell something and kick one of the tires hard.

Carissa.

Jasper sighed. The universe was clearly enjoying messing with him tonight.

He brought the car to a stop behind her black sedan and let out a long, frustrated exhale. Then he exited the car and walked to Carissa, who was covering her face with her hands.

"Everything okay?" he called out. Clearly, she hadn't heard him pull up, because she jumped a mile.

"Jasper," she said, placing a hand over her heart. "You scared the crap out of me. What are you doing here?"

Despite their surroundings, he couldn't help but inhale her perfume, a clean scent with just a hint of flowers. "I was just driving home and saw you on the side of the road."

Carissa's eyes flickered to his car and then back to him. "Out by yourself on a Saturday night?"

There was something about the way she asked the question that had his ire rising. "What if I am?"

"None of my business." Again, she glanced over at his car as if she was searching for something. Or someone. "I just heard you had a date tonight."

"You heard… From who?"

"Your mother."

He clamped down on the urge to roll his eyes. "Well, since you're so interested in my social life, yes, I was on a date."

She tossed her hair over her shoulder. "I don't care if

you were. I have bigger things to worry about than you and your libido."

"Let's leave my libido out of it. What's going on here?"

She deflated. "My car… I can't believe… I so don't need this right now."

She was flustered, an emotion he didn't often see her exhibit. Carissa was one of the most levelheaded women he knew. At least, she used to be. Her frustration got to him.

"Don't worry. I can help you change a tire."

"I know how to change a tire." He would have been impressed but he noticed she was nailing him with a furious stare. "What I don't know is what to do when your engine overheats." She pointed at the open hood.

"Ah. Well, that's different, then." He hadn't even noticed her hood or the smoke billowing from it.

She raised an eyebrow and tapped her foot.

He relented. "Okay, I don't know what to do, either. But I have a really great mechanic."

She laughed. "Well, that's something. Can we give him a call?"

"It's Saturday night. His shop closed at five."

She shook her head. "Of course. I didn't even think about that. I guess I'll call him first thing tomorrow morning."

Jasper's turn to shake his head. "Nope. Tomorrow's Sunday. They're not open. Most things aren't."

"Seriously? Where am I? Back in 1955?"

"You're back in Bayside."

She rolled her eyes. "Goody. The joys of small town living."

"There are advantages to small towns, too. I can call my mechanic at home and let him know what's going on. He's a good guy. He'll probably come tow your car to his shop tomorrow and it will be there first thing Monday morning. I can give you a ride home now."

She emitted a half cough, half laugh.

"What?" he asked.

"You want to drive me home? I thought our truce was over."

This time he let his eyes roll dramatically. "Are you seriously bringing that up at this moment? You're stranded and your aunt's cottage is only a couple minutes' drive from here. What's the big deal? I'm not going to let you stand here by yourself, especially at night. I mean, do you want to walk home by yourself in the dark?"

She looked around at the woods lining the road. The crickets were doing their best nighttime chirping. Other than that, there wasn't a sound. It was creepy. As if reading his thoughts, Carissa shivered.

"Fine," she relented.

While she grabbed her purse from the front seat and locked her doors, Jasper called his buddy from the garage and made arrangements for him to pick up Carissa's car. Then they walked back to his car.

"Nice car," she said, pointing at the red Porsche.

"Thanks. I always wanted one."

She joined him in the front seat. "It's certainly cozy in here."

What the heck? Did she not want to sit close to him? "Like I said, it's only a couple minutes' drive."

Who knew how long a couple minutes could feel? Sitting so near to her had his pulse skyrocketing. Between her heavenly scent and the sight of those long, shapely legs, he was finding it difficult to concentrate on the road.

"I probably should have just called Elle or Riley to come get me," she said under her breath, but loud enough for Jasper to hear.

"Honestly, Car, I was already right there. Good to see you're still stubborn."

She snorted. "Oh please. You are in no position to say I'm stubborn. You don't know what I'm like. You haven't seen me in ten years."

"Exactly." He banged his hand off the steering wheel. "Ten years with no contact."

Silence fell over the car. Jasper's words hung in the air.

"See," Carissa said quietly. "I told you. Dumb idea."

He hated to admit she was probably right. Luckily, they'd reached her house and he threw the Porsche in Park. Carissa practically bounded from the car.

"Thanks for the ride and for calling your mechanic," she said quickly and slammed the door.

Was she kidding him? Jasper yanked the keys from the ignition and bounded across the driveway that led to the front porch steps. "Car," he called. The air smelled of hamburgers and charcoal. Probably a Labor Day weekend barbecue.

She spun around, confusion on her face. "What?"

"You're going to just leave like that?" he asked.

"Yes," she said adamantly. "We're not on a date. In fact, you were on a date with someone else tonight. Where is she?"

He cocked his head and studied her. Her cheeks were flushed, her eyes bright. Realization dawned. "Are you… jealous?"

If her face was flushed before his question, it was on fire now. "Jealous? Excuse me?"

"Help me out, Car. Because I've never seen you like this before."

"You haven't seen me at all in ten years."

"Yeah, we've established that. Whose fault is that? Not mine."

She threw her arms in the air. "You have no idea what you're talking about. Go home, Jasper."

"You know, Car, a little gratitude would be nice."

She ground her teeth together. "Thank you so much, savior Jasper. I so appreciate it." Sarcasm coated each word.

"You are such a spoiled brat."

She put her hands on her hips. "You're a snobby playboy."

"Oh really?"

"Yeah, really," she said.

He groaned and ran a hand over his face. "What are we doing?"

"I think we're arguing."

He didn't want to ask, but at the same time, he couldn't stop the words from leaving his mouth. "What is your issue with me?"

She walked down one step. "My issue is that you kissed me only a matter of days ago. Tonight, you went on a date with another woman. And I know that I told you to keep dating and forget about our kiss," she continued in one breath. "And I also know that you have every reason to hate the fact that I'm back in town. But...but I can't help how I feel knowing you were on a date tonight."

"How do you feel?"

She blew out a loud breath. "Well, not good."

He leveled her with a stare. "That's not fair, Carissa."

She threw her hands in the air. "You think I don't know that? Of course it's not fair. It's completely irrational."

"I date a lot."

"Of course you do."

He took a step toward her. "What is that supposed to mean?"

"It means you're the golden boy, the life of the party."

He had no idea where that comment came from but he could see the strain in her eyes. "Are those bad things?"

"You have no idea."

"I think you're the one who has no idea. What did you think, Carissa? I wouldn't have a life? You broke up with me and disappeared. Did you think I would sit around pining for you for the rest of my days?"

The tides changed. A surprised expression crossed her face. "No, of course not," she said quietly.

"You got married. Really young, too. Did you honestly think I wouldn't be with other women?"

"I didn't really think…"

"No, you didn't. You just dumped me and ran away."

"Jasper, wait."

"No." He started walking away with long, determined strides. Then he realized he needed to stop and face her. He'd waited too long, held the words back for too many years. So he turned back.

"You know, it wasn't bad enough that you broke up with me. But it came out of nowhere. We'd been to the movies the night before. Remember?" He didn't wait for her to comment. "The next day, it was over. And that wasn't the worst part. Do you know what was?"

Her eyes had widened and her arms had woven around her stomach protectively as she bit her lip. She shook her head.

"You were my friend. We'd known each other our entire lives. We'd been in the same circle since before we could even remember. And you just left. Without warning. Do you know how hard that was on me? It felt like you had died."

"Oh, Jasper."

He clenched his fingers into a tight fist as the years of pent up anger and hurt washed over him. "You told me that I wasn't good enough."

She sucked in a harsh breath and walked to him. "I never said that."

"Might as well have said it. All I did know was that I

was this eighteen-year-old kid who had been overlooked by his parents time after time. I was never good enough for them. Cam was the heir. I was just extra. But with you, I was someone. Until you took that away. Because I wasn't good enough for you, either."

She closed her eyes and a pained expression shadowed her face and those gorgeous features. He watched her take a deep breath. "You reminded me of my father and that scared the hell out of me," she said so softly he almost didn't hear.

His anger deflated. Carissa had never had a great relationship with her dad. He'd never understood all the particulars but he'd witnessed more than a fair share of fighting between the two of them. It hadn't been the usual teen versus parent butting of heads, either. There was something deeper there. Even as a kid, he'd realized that.

She closed the distance between them and took his face in her hands, forcing him to meet her gaze. "Listen to me, Jasper Dumont. I was a selfish, scared eighteen-year-old girl. And my life hasn't turned out so great. But you," she lightly shook his head. "Look at everything you've accomplished. You were always good enough. I was the one who made a mistake."

"You still left."

Sadness filled her eyes as she nodded. "It didn't have anything to do with you, Jasp. It was me. All me."

It seemed like she wanted to tell him more, say something else. While Jasper wanted to know, wanted to know everything, he also feared hearing it. Afraid that she could say something that would seep in and hurt him again. So he did the only thing he could think to do. He retreated into himself.

"Jasper, look at me." She shook him. "Dammit, don't do that. I broke up with you because of my issues, not yours."

She had no idea about his issues. About how he never allowed people to get close enough to hurt him. He was still the life of the party but from a very safe, very self-imposed distance. His manner of thinking was that you could have fun with people, but as soon as you truly let them in, you gave them the power. Once someone had power over you, they could squash you.

Just like she'd done.

Suddenly, he felt tired. The exhaustion allowed his guard to slip. Just a bit.

Carissa must have sensed this. "Jasp," she whispered. As if she desperately wanted to show him his importance, she pressed her lips to his. As soon as her lips touched his, he was helpless to do anything but kiss her back. Slowly, he felt himself coming back from the dark place he'd just been. The dark place he rarely allowed himself to go.

She nipped at his lower lip and he sucked in a breath. He pulled her closer to him, reaching for the back of her head so he could angle her better. His tongue dived into her mouth as she clutched at his shirt.

They were so in sync. Every nip, bite, kiss, tease, moan, was shared until they were both left breathing heavily, staring into each other's eyes, wondering what had just transpired between them.

Pressing his forehead to hers, he took a moment. Needed a moment. But clarity didn't come.

He didn't know how long they stood like that, heads pressed together, breath mingling, arms wound around each other. But he did know that he felt like a huge weight had been lifted from his shoulders. Carissa had admitted her fault in their breakup.

She sighed.

"What's wrong?" he asked.

"We really should stop doing this."

Jasper agreed. Wholeheartedly. Because if he kept kissing her, he didn't know if he'd ever be the same again. "You're right," he whispered.

She turned and retreated to the front door. When she reached it, she looked back, biting her lip, as she waved good-night.

Yes, they definitely had to stop kissing. And yet… Jasper wasn't sure if he could.

Chapter Seven

Quite a few people saw Jasper Dumont on a date at the Boat House with Simone Graves last Saturday night. But he somehow ended the evening in the driveway of Carissa Blackwell's cottage. My spies heard them arguing, until they didn't hear anything at all. Hmm, wonder what those two old lovebirds were doing? Leave a comment if you think "Casper" (which won by a landslide over on Twitter) is happening!

In related news, you're never going to guess what I found out about Carissa Blackwell's ex-husband...

In theory, catering Mrs. Dumont's tea party seemed like a great idea. But as Carissa glanced around her aunt's kitchen, she wasn't feeling 100 percent confident.

"You can do this," she said aloud.

And she knew she could do it. At least, she hoped so. She'd thrown dozens of parties for her husband's colleagues and friends, but nothing of this caliber. Mrs. Dumont was holding a ladies' tea for one of her charities that provided scholarships for local high school students. There was also a silent auction to raise even more money.

In Chicago, Preston had wanted her as involved with the local charities as possible. It was the perfect combination. She provided the food and he wrote a big, fat check. She'd catered teas, luncheons, brunches, costume parties, swanky dinners and more.

Then, why was she feeling so nervous? Perhaps because she'd gotten up at four in the morning to bake scones. Or maybe it was the three cups of coffee she'd consumed while the scones were in the oven and she began assembling the tea sandwiches, icing the mini cupcakes, putting the finishing touches on the fruit platters, and fixing the large containers of lemonade and iced tea.

The kitchen smelled of baking, that wonderful aroma of sugars and spices merging together. She'd put orange zest into one batch of scones, and that fresh citrus scent set her mouth to watering.

She just wanted everything to be perfect. She let out an exhausted chuckle. If someone walked into the house at this moment, *perfect* would probably not be the word that came to mind. Ingredients were spread throughout the room. Pots and pans and other kitchen utensils littered the counters. Of course, her aunt's kitchen wasn't the largest room she'd ever cooked in. But hey, it had gotten the job done. Now she just needed to load her newly fixed car and make herself a little more presentable.

Spotting her car sitting out in the driveway, she didn't even want to think about the bill she'd just received on that. But at least she wouldn't break down again on the side of the road only to be rescued by Jasper.

Jasper.

She stopped in her packing and leaned back against the counter. Absentmindedly, she tapped a finger against her lips as she remembered how it had felt to kiss him the other night.

She'd meant what she'd told him. She had been selfish when she'd broken up with him. She'd never really thought about how he took her words that day. Maybe because she didn't want to let herself think about it. Maybe now she needed to tell him the full story. Why she'd really dumped him that day.

She began stacking cupcakes in her special travel container. Still, she couldn't stop thinking about Jasper. She'd been back for a week and kissed him twice. There hadn't been any real closure the other night in her driveway and maybe that was a good thing. She needed time to think and decide what she wanted to do. Because on the one hand, she desperately craved her independence. But on the other, the feel of Jasper's mouth against hers sent waves of pleasure through her days later.

An hour later Carissa was parking in the back of the Dumont estate, near the kitchen. Some of the staff appeared to help her carry everything inside. Mrs. Dumont told her they would hold the event in the atrium, a part of the house she'd always adored back in high school. It seemed so fancy and sophisticated with its glass walls, pretty decor and dainty furniture. Who else had an atrium in their home?

The next two hours were a total blur. Between setting up the food and the arrival of Bayside's most charitable women, Carissa was too busy to be nervous.

Of course, her mother used to run with this crowd, so there were quite a few reunions and hugs. There were even more questions about her parents. She'd expected that though and did a fairly good job of evading the queries and seamlessly switching topics.

As her part of the job wound down, she did a quiet lap of the perimeter of the atrium. The women seemed to be enjoying the event. She'd displayed the food on tiered trays provided by Mrs. Dumont. One layer held the sandwiches, the next had the scones, and chocolate-covered strawberries and shortbread cookies sat on the top. Waiters served the cold beverages plus Mrs. Dumont's prized tea collection.

As Carissa reached the back of the room, she noticed that the silent auction was doing quite well. Having had to provide her own college tuition, she appreciated that the ladies of Bayside were raising money for such a worthy cause.

"Ohmigod, your scones are to die for." Carissa smiled as Riley rushed over to her. "Where did you learn to make these?"

"My aunt Val taught me when I was thirteen. The shortbread cookies are her recipe, as well."

Riley's face grew serious. "Listen, we are having a fundraiser for the high school next month. It's to raise money for the different sports teams. Cheerleading is one of them."

Carissa had been a cheerleader back in high school. She liked the idea of raising money for any sports programs.

"It's going to be a huge event," Riley continued. "There's going to be a raffle, a huge bake sale, and—wait for it," she said dramatically. "We're holding a date auction."

Carissa groaned. "Please don't ask me to go up for auction. I'm damaged goods right now. Seriously, I don't think you would get fifty cents for me."

Riley frowned. "You're not damaged goods. You got divorced. Half of the people who get married end up splitting."

Carissa relented. Riley always did have a way to cut to the chase. "I suppose you're right. But I'd still rather not have people bid on me."

"Don't worry. The auction is for the men of Bayside. So bring your wallet. Jasper's going to be up on the auction block." She wiggled her eyebrows.

Carissa almost let out a sigh at his name. Then she silently admonished herself. Since when was the mention of Jasper enough to have her stomach twisting into knots and leave her with the idea to keep sighing over and over like some Victorian-era damsel?

"I'll keep that in mind. Anyway, did you need some help with the high school fund-raiser?"

"Yes." Riley's emerald green eyes were practically sparkling. "Would you mind doing some baking? We can't pay you, of course. But I'd really appreciate it. Usually, Myrtle, who owns the bakery in town, makes hundreds and hundreds of cookies. But since the tourist season is over, she's taking a long vacation."

"No problem. I'd love to help out."

They chatted a little longer, agreeing to meet up later that night with Elle for cocktails. Then Carissa made her way back to the kitchen to begin the arduous task of cleaning up.

"A job very well done." Carissa looked up from packing the utensils she'd brought from her personal collection to see a glowing Mrs. Dumont enter the kitchen.

"Thank you."

"I had several women ask me for your information, so I suspect you'll get some jobs from this one."

Carissa crossed the room. "I can't thank you enough for trusting me, not once, but twice. I appreciate it so much."

"My pleasure." Mrs. Dumont peered deeply into her eyes. Then she pushed a strand of Carissa's hair behind her ear in a very maternal and comforting gesture before cupping her cheek. She stared into Carissa's eyes for a long time, a caring expression on her face. "You've been through a lot, haven't you?"

"No more than other people," Carissa admitted honestly, even though she wanted to scream, *yes, I'm hurting*.

She patted Carissa's cheek. "True, everyone goes

through hard times. But it's different when it happens to you. I'm always here if you need to talk."

After a long look, Mrs. Dumont started walking away and Carissa was left standing in the kitchen wondering what in the heck had just transpired between them. Without overthinking it, she called out.

"Mrs. Dumont," she waited for the woman to turn back to her. "There's a reason for it." Mrs. Dumont cocked her head to the side. "There's a reason why my parents left town. I'm sure you've been wondering. You were all so close."

Lilah seemed contemplative before speaking. "I always suspected there was."

"There's a reason why I broke up with Jasper, too."

Lilah nodded. "That's not a surprise, either. I also suspect that the two things are connected somehow." She pinned Carissa with a stare. "Am I right?"

"Yes," she whispered. "I'm not really ready to talk—"

Mrs. Dumont held her hand up. "If and when you're ready, you know where to find me."

"Thank you. I just wanted you to know that, because you've been so kind to me."

And because I kissed your son again the other night. But she didn't dare say that out loud. Instead, she accepted Mrs. Dumont's kind smile as she continued out of the room.

Carissa tried to pack up more of her things but it was tough with all the thoughts running through her head. She couldn't help but think about her parents. They had spent so much time at this house when she was growing up. She wondered what they would think about her walking these halls as the hired help instead of their privileged daughter.

When she pushed her anger aside, she felt sad for them. It must have been difficult to go from one extreme lifestyle to the other.

Then she shook her head. They'd done it to themselves. At least, her father had with his mismanagement of money and foolish investments. If that weren't bad enough, they'd practically hightailed it out of town in the middle of the night. Not a word to their friends, to good people like the Dumonts whom they'd spent so much time with.

An image of getting into her car in the wee hours of dawn and driving out of Chicago filled her mind. Carissa bit her lip. *It's not the same.* Right?

"You look like you're in deep thought."

She jumped at the sound of Riley's voice. "Hi. I didn't hear you come in." She noticed Riley's pinched expression. "What's up, Ri?"

"Um…" Riley took her hand. "I'm really sorry, Carissa."

The hairs on the back of Carissa's neck stood up at full attention. "You're sorry? What in the world for?"

Even though they were the only two people in the kitchen, Riley still glanced around the room before lowering her voice. "I didn't realize that your husband, er, your ex-husband that is—"

"What about him?" Carissa interrupted.

"You didn't tell me that he cheated on you."

All of the cakes she'd been sampling, the goodies she'd been nibbling on throughout the day, sank into one heavy stone at the bottom of her stomach. She knew she couldn't keep her divorce quiet, but dammit, she'd wanted to keep the cheating part out of the mix. Wasn't it embarrassing enough that she had to endure the end of a marriage?

"I, I…well…"

Riley kept going. "It sucks. I've had boyfriends cheat on me before. And when I lived in New York, well, let's just say that I understand how you feel."

Now she was curious about what in the hell happened when Riley lived in New York. But it was only a fleeting distraction. Carissa was still reeling that Riley knew any of this. Then something clicked. Oh no. The realization slapped her in the face. Riley wasn't the only one who knew about this.

"Riley, please tell me you didn't find out about my ex from the Bayside freaking Blogger."

"Well…"

"You've gotta be kidding me." She kicked at one of the crates she'd used to haul the food in. "She wrote a blog about my divorce? About Preston?"

"Actually, she was also tweeting about it." Riley looked contrite.

"How in the hell would she even find out?" If she thought she felt a stone sinking in her stomach before, it was like all of Stonehenge just landed hard in her midsection. There was only one time she'd spoken about the affair. Only one person she'd divulged that information to.

"Carissa, are you okay?" Riley asked. "You look a little pale."

Okay? She's wasn't okay. But at least she was no longer feeling sad. Now she was pissed at the person who had revealed her secret to the Bayside Blogger.

Jasper Dumont.

Jasper was feeling pretty damn good. He'd had a great day in the office. All of the meetings he'd attended that afternoon promised exciting opportunities for Dumont Incorporated.

He crossed to his bar and poured a glass of his favorite scotch. Taking the glass to the windows, he took a moment to soak in the scene below. The sun still shone brightly, even as it would shortly be making its descent. Soon, the sky would become a mix of brilliant colors, reflecting over the bobbing ships and boats docked in the bay.

Some high school kids were down in the square, fooling around, just being kids. He remembered those days well. School had started back up the day before and it would take a little while longer before they remembered they hated school. For now, the excitement over being reunited with friends, upcoming Friday night football games, and new school supplies was running rampant.

The kids entered The Brewside, a luxury he didn't have back in high school. Ten years ago, an old used bookstore stood in the café's spot. He'd spent a lot of time there. It was the only place in town where you could grab a coffee and hang out. No one rushed them. It was really chill.

His favorite thing to peruse were graphic novels. He gave a quick glance at the bookshelves in his condo. Carissa had noticed his collection the other day.

He could hear Carissa in his head now, as if it were a decade ago.

"I don't get it. They're just a bunch of dumb comic books. I didn't realize I was dating a comic book geek."

"No, no, no. They are graphic novels and that makes them infinitely more cool."

She, on the other hand, was forever flipping through the pages of fashion magazines and cookbooks. He should have realized back then she'd go into the cooking field.

Jasper shook the liquid around in his glass as he considered their old hangout. A bookstore. Something Bayside didn't currently have. Of course, brick-and-mortar bookstores were risky businesses these days. But he liked a challenge. He grabbed his iPad and made a few notes. Then he glanced down at the square again. Yes, definitely something to consider. If he could think of something else to pair the bookstore with, it would be easier to get the funding. Maybe a bookstore with a café inside. A café that would need catering help. Which led right back to Carissa Blackwell.

He'd managed to keep thoughts of Carissa at bay for most of the day. He'd decided to give her some space. After their kiss the other night, he thought she might need some room.

"Ah, hell," he said. He was the one who really needed space. They'd delved into very sensitive territory. After all these years, he'd never dreamed that he'd actually get to have a conversation with her about it.

The truth was, she'd really hurt him all those years ago. Getting to voice that hurt went a long way to healing an old and very potent wound.

Then they'd kissed.

He sucked in a breath at the memory of her lips on his, at the little sounds she made, at the way she felt in his arms.

Jasper wasn't an idiot. He knew the very best thing would be for him to keep his distance. Go back to his usual dating pattern. There were plenty of women out there.

But only one stunning blonde who could kiss him senseless.

A loud knock sounded at his front door, pulling him from his musings. Jasper put down his glass of scotch and crossed the room. When he opened the door, he was shocked to see the very person he'd just been thinking about. But there she was, her thick hair cascading over her shoulders, her gray eyes alert and bright. Her face was flushed.

"Carissa," he said with surprise in his voice.

Jasper was thrilled to see her at his door. But taking a long look at her gave him the feeling that this was not a happy visit. Unless the smoke coming out of her ears was actually glitter. Those red cheeks were apparently not from the exertion of walking down the hallway to his door.

Nope. She had her mad on. And he had a feeling she would be sharing that mad with him momentarily.

"Can I come in?" she asked around a clenched jaw.

"Of course." He held the door open farther and allowed her to pass into the room. "Can I get you a drink?"

He decided to make himself comfortable by sitting back in his favorite leather recliner. He gestured to the other chair and the couch but she simply moved to stand directly in front of him, arms crossed over her chest.

"What the hell, Jasper?" she said, her voice exploding into the quiet room.

Like a firework being set off into the night sky, her temper roared into the stratosphere and then quickly dissipated back down to Earth. She deflated, her shoulders collapsing and a frown appearing on her face. In a split second her anger had morphed into sadness.

He rose from his chair. "What's wrong, Car?"

Her eyes held a mix of confusion and worry. "The Bayside Blogger. Does that ring any bells?"

Not what he'd been expecting her to say. Of course, he really had no idea where she was going with this. "I haven't read her column today. What did she say?"

"That I got divorced because my husband cheated on me. That's what she said." Her voice broke on the last word.

He leaned forward. His heart went out to her. That couldn't have been easy to read. Now the entire town would realize what she'd went through, and knowing Carissa, she definitely wouldn't want any pity. Or take kindly to her very personal business being out in the public realm.

"I'm sorry, Car."

Her lip quivered. She pointed at him in question. "Jasper, did you tell her?"

He wasn't sure what she meant. "Did I tell who what?"

"Did you tell the Bayside Blogger, whoever she is, that Preston cheated on me?" The anger in her words was clear.

An icy cold feeling seeped through his body. "You're asking me if I told a gossip columnist about your ex-husband and your personal marriage problems?"

She nodded. "I'm sorry, Jasp, but I have to ask."

Was she kidding him? "Carissa Blackwell, you've known me my entire life. I can't believe you would come over here and ask me that."

Her gaze darted around the room and then she pushed her hands through her hair. "If it wasn't you, then who else? Process of elimination. You are literally the only person I told about, about…the cheating." She lowered her voice when she said the word *cheating*.

He felt for her. He did. But he was having a hard time remembering that fact when she was standing in his living room insulting him.

"For you to accuse me—"

She quickly cut him off. "I'm not accusing you, Jasper. I'm simply asking."

"It's never simple with you."

She rolled her eyes, which filled with anger once again. Fine with him. He'd rather have her mad than sad.

"And it's always so dramatic with you," she countered. "It's a logical conclusion for me to reach."

She'd hurt him that day she'd dumped him all those years ago. And she was hurting him again today. After their conversation the other night, he thought they'd at least taken a step forward. But this accusation pushed them quite a few steps back.

Jasper's temper didn't flare often. He was a master at staying calm and cool. But he was having a hell of a struggle keeping composed at the moment. He took a step toward her and she held her ground. "Listen to me. I did not tell the Bayside Blogger, or anyone else for that matter, about your marriage, your divorce, or any other details about you. No one, Carissa."

She tossed her head up, meeting his gaze. "How else do you explain it?"

"I can't. I don't know how the Blogger finds out the information she does. Or he does. But I swear on everything that I hold dear that I did not out you."

She paced a few steps toward the window and then back again. Her mouth opened and it seemed like she was about to say something. But she quickly shut it. Then she paced again before finally landing in front of him. She whispered, "My divorce is the single most embarrassing event of my life."

That comment took the wind out of his sails. "A lot of people get divorced, Car."

"Riley said the same thing. And I know it's true. A lot of people get cheated on, too," she said in a shaky voice. "I was fine knowing that everyone in Bayside would learn of my divorce. But the reason for it..."

He hated seeing her like this. She'd always been good at keeping her emotions in check. It used to impress him back in high school. She had some of the greatest control he'd ever seen. And she was much easier to deal with when she was laughing or angry or yelling at him. But as a tear formed in her eye, threatening to fall, Jasper reached for the only lifeboat he could find. Unfortunately, it wasn't to comfort, but to antagonize.

"I understand that. I do. But for you to come in here, guns blazing, and start blaming me for something that is pretty repulsive is not okay. Maybe the real problem is that you didn't really take the time to get to know me back then, because you sure as hell don't know me now."

"Jasper—"

"Before you say something else that is sure to outrage me, I suggest you go."

"But I only meant to—"

Again, he cut her off. "You walked away from me all those years ago. Maybe you should do it again right now."

He turned his back on her and walked to the kitchen. He waited until he heard his front door close. As usual, his anger dissipated quickly and he was left with a raw, hollow feeling.

He hadn't meant to bring up their past. In fact, he didn't really know where that even came from. Maybe he'd been holding it in for far too many years. Maybe it needed to be said. In any case, it hadn't helped matters. He didn't blame Carissa for being upset about the Bayside Blogger's reveal of her ex-husband's infidelity. But taking it out on him was not the answer.

Perhaps his original idea of giving her space and time hadn't been so crazy. He should probably give her even more because he sure as hell needed some himself.

Carissa was a mess. She'd been a mess since Riley first told her about the Bayside Blogger's article. She'd become even more of a mess after she got home and read the article herself. But what just happened with Jasper might have put her over the edge.

She kept racking her brain but she was positive she hadn't told anyone else about Preston's cheating. Only Jasper. But when she'd brought it to Jasper's attention—okay, accused him, because that's really what she'd done. Accused him with guns blazing. When she'd done that, the look on his face had been heartbreaking. If he'd been just plain old angry, she could have dealt with that. But it had been hurt that crossed his handsome face. Not anger.

More than that, he was clearly still holding on to their breakup. And she couldn't blame him for that. It might be time to finally reveal the whole story to him. That is, if he would ever even talk to her again.

She pushed her hand through her hair. She'd been up since four this morning. She needed a shower. A good stiff drink wouldn't hurt anything, either. And she'd definitely like to be off her feet.

Her phone alerted her to a text message from Riley.

Where are you? Cocktails with me and Elle, remember? Boat House. Now.

Damn. Well, at least she would get that stiff drink.

Carissa had been wandering around the streets of Bayside aimlessly, trying to decipher this mystery. Luckily, she wasn't far from the Boat House, the upscale restaurant right on the water. They had excellent seafood, a nice ambience, and according to Riley, a great bar and lounge area. Apparently, Riley and Elle met for cocktails there quite frequently. If she wasn't so emotionally exhausted, it would have touched her to be included.

She pushed open the door and her stomach growled at the enticing smell of salty seafood, fresh bread and melted butter. She stole a quick glance around. Looked as if they'd renovated the place from what she remembered. It looked good. The bar area was cute with high tables and tall wooden chairs. The entire restaurant seemed abuzz with activity.

She easily spotted her friends and made her way toward their table. They both waved as she approached.

"I'm sorry," Carissa said. "I lost track of time."

"No wonder. I heard you had quite the day," Elle said, pushing a glass of water toward her.

Carissa slumped in her chair. "It was awful. I went over to Jasper's and blamed him for the whole situation with the Bayside Blogger because he's the only person I told about it. But then he turned it on me somehow. I'm not even sure how. He made me feel awful and you know what? I deserved it. And then he kicked me out and now I feel doubly horrible."

Both Riley's and Elle's mouths were hanging open as they stared at her. Finally, Elle spoke. "I was actually referring to the ladies' tea you catered, which Lilah said was a huge success."

"But you were clearly busy after that," Riley added with a twinkle in her eye. "We definitely need to discuss."

A perky young waitress bounced over to their table, wearing a black skirt and a crisp white blouse. "Drinks?"

"Hells yeah," Riley said. "We've been waiting for you to order, Carissa. A round of cosmos and keep 'em coming," she said to the waitress.

Both women leaned in as Carissa spilled the whole situation.

"But you see, right? It had to be Jasper. Because he's the only person I told about Preston."

"Not necessarily," Elle said.

"What do you mean?" Carissa asked as she finished off her cosmo.

"It's crazy," Riley said. "The Bayside Blogger just knows stuff. No matter how hard you try to keep something a secret, she finds out. Last year, I was dating someone who lived about thirty minutes away. We had a horrible breakup. In his town. Not a soul from Bayside in sight. And yet the next morning, there it was splashed across her blog."

Elle nodded. "When I first returned last spring, I was in her stupid column every day. Not to mention all the Twitter discussions."

Carissa's jaw dropped. "Really?"

Riley finished her drink, as well. "Yep. It's awful. No matter what you do or where you go, there she is. She's probably in this restaurant right now."

The waitress stopped by their table. "Another round?"

"Yes," all three of them answered in unison.

The waitress widened her eyes, but replied, "Okeydokey."

"So see," Elle continued, "Jasper may very well be innocent in all of this."

"Oh God." Carissa moaned as she ran a hand over her face. "If that's true then I'm a huge witch."

The waitress, who had returned with their second round of drinks, froze, giving Carissa a wary once-over.

"Don't worry, sweetie. She won't be a witch," Riley said amiably.

"We're also very good tippers," Elle added, and the waitress seemed appeased. Still, she did ask if they wanted to order any appetizers but didn't actually wait around for their response.

"See what I mean?" Carissa pointed toward her. "I'm scaring off innocent young waitresses now."

Riley snorted. "Oh, she'll be fine."

"And Jasper will be fine, too." Elle put her drink down on the table. "I really don't think he would betray your confidence and reveal something so personal to the town gossip columnist. Besides, what would he have gained by doing something like that? Seems to me like he's trying hard to get back in your good graces."

Carissa bit her lip. "Jeez, when you put it like that it makes me feel like an idiot for even going over there."

"You shouldn't," Riley said. "He was the only one you told. Makes sense to jump to that conclusion."

Seems to me like he's trying hard to get back in your good graces. Elle's words repeated in her head. Carissa wondered if that was true. It didn't seem like it the other night when he was on a date with some other woman. Of course, he did help with her car and drive her home. And then there was the very sultry, very passionate kiss they'd shared…

"Can I ask a question?" Carissa said suddenly. "Jasper isn't married."

"That's not a question," Riley pointed out.

Carissa played with a strand of her hair, twisting it around her finger. "He's not dating anyone, either."

Riley chuckled. "Still not a question. But I think I know what you're trying to ask. You want to know about Jasper's dating history."

"I mean, not in extreme detail, but I am curious. He's gorgeous and charming. Not to mention, he's incredibly wealthy. He runs his family's freaking business. He's a catch."

"Careful," Riley said. "One might think you're still interested."

She ignored Riley's comment. "It's just, with all those qualifications, I would think a line of women would be following him everywhere."

Elle smiled. "Oh, they do. Trust me. He dated someone named Mindy for a couple months when I first got back. I thought it might be serious, but they broke up."

"Of course they did." Riley took a sip of her drink and looked pensive. "He always breaks up with them. Have you noticed?" she asked Elle.

Elle nodded. "According to Cam, Jasper never stays with the same woman for more than a few months."

Carissa was shocked. "Never?"

"Nope," Riley said.

"Not in college?"

"Not that I know of," Riley answered.

"But…" Carissa sat back in her chair, considering. "That would mean I was the last long-term girlfriend he had." She looked to her friends, who exchanged a glance and nodded. "But there must have been someone he was serious about."

Elle took a moment before answering. "I don't want to make you feel worse than you already do, but I think Jasper is afraid of getting hurt."

"So he never lets anyone get close enough to hurt him." *Except me*, Carissa thought with sadness. What did she do? Hurt him at the first chance. "I feel so stupid," she admitted.

"You shouldn't," Elle said, loyalty in her voice.

"Thanks, but I do. For so many things, so many choices I've made over the years." Carissa reached for her glass but didn't actually take a sip. "When I walked in and found Preston with that woman, I wasn't that surprised. I had a feeling he'd been cheating on me for a while. That's when I got my proof."

"Well, you divorced his sorry ass. So you win." Riley toasted her.

But Carissa shook her head. "I wish I had. But in the end, Preston was the one to request a divorce." Admitting this secret felt liberating. She'd been holding it in for far too long. "I'd become so apathetic."

"About your marriage?" Elle asked.

"About everything. About my marriage, my life, my lack of a career." Her stomach clenched. She'd become her father. Living off of someone else's money and success. She'd become the one thing she'd swore she'd never be. That was the embarrassing part. That's what she really didn't want anyone to know.

Ashamed, she glanced at her friends through her eyelashes. "Pretty pathetic, huh?"

This was the moment they could agree. What shocked her was that they didn't.

"Kind of the opposite of pathetic," Elle said. Riley agreed. "I mean, if I were in your position I would probably be hiding under a rock somewhere crying my eyes out, shoving Double Stuf Oreos in my mouth and being scared out of my mind. But you came here and you're starting your own business."

"That takes cojones." Riley lifted her drink again. "Let's toast to that. To your new life, Carissa Blackwell, and to your big ole cojones."

Overwhelmed, Carissa pushed down the ball that had formed in her throat. She raised her glass and touched it to her friends'.

Maybe it was finally time for new beginnings. Only, she had to say goodbye to her past first.

Chapter Eight

For someone with almost no experience in the catering field, Carissa Blackwell has managed to pull off two yummy events so far here in town. Too bad she can't enjoy her success with Jasper, because I've heard that our resident Ross and Rachel are taking a break...again. What could be the cause this time? Dear readers, I certainly hope it wasn't something I said!

Carissa hadn't apologized to Jasper yet. She'd thought about it. A lot. She still didn't know how the Bayside Blogger had found out her ex-husband had cheated on her. She supposed the Blogger could have just Googled her. In any case, she knew that she owed Jasper an apology for flying off the handle.

She told herself she hadn't called him because she'd been devoting every waking hour to her new business, which was true. With Elle's artistic help, she'd designed a logo for Save the Day Catering and was able to order business cards. She'd even started a website, including some sample menus and a list of the types of events she was available for. It was pretty basic as far as websites went, but it would do the trick for now. She had plans to start photographing her food and adding pictures and descriptions.

Once she had more jobs under her belt she could consider a marketing campaign. Right now, word of mouth would have to suffice, but eventually she'd like to make up flyers or postcards, offer discounts and specials, and maybe one day, hire some help.

Because of the successful ladies' tea, she'd received three more jobs. Since she now had Mrs. Dumont as a reference, she no longer had to worry on that score. Besides, no one else in Bayside realized that she hadn't been a professional caterer back in Chicago. As far as Carissa was concerned, her informal experience was helping her just fine.

She'd set up a makeshift office in the living room. Or tried to. Currently, she was sitting on the floor between the couch and the coffee table, trying to organize the files she'd recently created. Just a couple more folders and color-coded labels and she would be on her way.

She let out a long sigh of relief. She could do this. She *would* do this. She wouldn't end up like her father and she would never rely on a man—or any person—ever again. She would keep full control of her life and no one else would be able to take it away from her again.

Bayside Blogger—check now.

At the sight of Elle's text message, Carissa's heart sank. This couldn't be good news. It wasn't as if the Bayside Blogger would report something happy about her. Like, "Oh that Carissa Blackwell has amazing hair and is really killing it as a caterer."

She quickly grabbed her laptop from the couch and pulled up the—she hated to admit it—bookmarked page on the *Bugle*'s website. As her eyes quickly scanned the contents of today's blog, Carissa didn't read anything that caused alarm. It was annoying, sure.

She was about to text Elle back, but then she reread the blog. The first time, she'd concentrated on the part about her and Jasper being compared to Ross and Rachel from *Friends*. That was enough to make her snort.

But on second glance, she homed in on the opening sentence. "For someone with almost no experience in the catering field…"

Carissa felt like someone was simultaneously extracting all the air from her lungs.

Oh no. Oh no. Oh no. This could not be happening. She paced away from her computer and then promptly returned to reread the blog a third time.

She'd been outed. Again. Damn, damn and double damn. She eyed the stack of business cards she'd just ordered. What was everyone in Bayside going to think? More importantly, how did the Bayside Blogger even find out about this? She'd told no one about her lack of experience. Not Elle, not Riley. Not even…

Jasper.

She rubbed her eyes as a tension headache began. Elle and Riley had been right the other night. They'd said that the Bayside Blogger just knew things. Things that no one else was privy to. Carissa hadn't told Jasper about her lack of experience in catering and yet, here it was in the gossip column anyway.

Carissa pulled up Twitter and started reading through the Bayside Blogger's recent tweets and replies.

Bayside Blogger @BSBlogger

My latest column's up at the @BSBugle site.

Judy Fashley @jdmfash
OMG! Jasper & Carissa broke up AGAIN?!?! @BSBlogger

Harry P. Belding @bocceball
RT @tdmfash They broke up? Didn't know they were dating. The real scoop is that C doesn't have much catering experience.

Reva Lewis @RLLight
Just read @BSBlogger's column. I wouldn't give C.B. my business, that's 4 sure.

Gertie Ward @gertieward26
Big reveal today on @BSBlogger. Although... I had her food at the Dumonts. It was yummy!

Carissa's first instinct was to scream, loud and long. Instead, she paced to the window, took a few deep breaths and then let out an oath. Why did people always make it seem like taking a couple deep inhales would change the way you feel? It never worked with her. She eyed a bottle of wine she'd picked up the other day. Now, there was a better solution for calming herself.

But in the end, Carissa filled a glass with water and sat at the small table in her aunt's kitchen. Perspective. That's what she needed. It was a stupid blog on a small town newspaper's website. How many people really read this article anyway? More importantly, how many people cared? She couldn't imagine that someone would deny her business simply because a blogger wrote an article about her. Right? Then, why was she starting to feel nauseous?

Her phone rang and she saw Elsie Reynolds's name on the display. Carissa was going to be catering her daughter's bridal shower in two weeks. If that went well, she held high hopes that she would be chosen as the caterer for the wedding reception. A wedding would be a major coup at this point.

"Carissaaaa," Mrs. Reynolds said, drawing out her name. "I just happened to be at the store shopping for favors for Bonnie's shower and someone directed me to the Bayside Blogger's website."

Of course they did. Carissa tried to remain calm. "Oh really?"

"Is it true, dear?"

Debating how she should play this, in the end, Carissa chose the truth. "It is a correct statement to say that I don't have any official training in catering. As in," she quickly continued, "I never worked for a caterer or had a business of my own."

"Now, see, dear, that is a problem. We've already invited over a hundred people to Bonnie's shower and everyone is expecting this to be an amazing event."

"Of course." Carissa was close to losing it.

"I just don't think I can continue on with you."

Mrs. Reynolds's dismissal hurt. All of Carissa's hard work and she was going to lose this important job. She was going to fail. Just like her father.

Then something snapped inside her. She wasn't like her father at all. Hadn't she already decided that? Maybe her dad would give up at this point. Cut his losses and move on. But if she truly wanted to be independent, truly make it on her own, bumps in the road were inevitable. This was her first test and she so wasn't failing this exam.

"I got this." She didn't realize she'd said the words out loud until Mrs. Reynolds questioned her.

"Excuse me?"

"Sorry," Carissa said. "Mrs. Reynolds, I completely understand your concerns about me."

"I'm glad you do."

"However, while I may not have official experience as a caterer, trust me when I say that I've been catering events for years, oftentimes at the last minute. In fact, there was a point when I was throwing at least one dinner party a week. In addition to that, I've trained with some of the best culinary instructors in Chicago."

"Yes, dear, but your references…"

"Lilah Dumont can serve as my reference. Besides, you were at both her end-of-summer party and the charity event she hosted last week. I think it's safe to say that my food spoke for itself."

"Well, of course, it was fabulous, but…"

Carissa was on a roll now. "Again, I understand and appreciate your concerns. I would feel the same way if I were in your shoes."

"You would?" Mrs. Reynolds's voice softened.

"Of course. This is your daughter's bridal shower. A once-in-a-lifetime event." *Unless precious Bonnie gets divorced like me*, Carissa thought wryly. "This day needs to be special, memorable."

"Exactly."

"And I think the menu we've chosen will go beyond meeting her expectations. I dare say that Bonnie is going to love what you have planned."

Mrs. Reynolds was teetering now. Carissa could feel it. Time to go in for the kill. "However, as insurance, I'm willing to offer you a twenty percent discount off the price we discussed. Plus, if you don't like the food or you're unhappy with my services, I will give you a full refund."

Carissa's palms began to sweat while she waited for the reply. Not only because of Mrs. Reynolds's possible answer but because taking a hit on this large party would not help her very fragile bottom line.

"This all sounds very reasonable, Carissa," Mrs. Reynolds finally said. "Okay, we have a deal."

"Great. I'll email you a revised contract as soon as we get off the phone."

After they hung up and Carissa sent off the new paperwork, she sat back in her seat. The 20 percent discount hurt, but not as much as losing the business altogether. Besides, she knew Mrs. Reynolds, her daughter and all the guests at the shower would love her culinary creations.

She bit her lip as she considered what had just transpired. She'd single-handedly saved the day. More than that, she'd taken her first step toward independence. No one else got her out of that jam. She'd done that herself.

"Go me," she said into the empty kitchen, which she followed up with a happy dance.

She felt good. In fact, she felt inspired to make some other changes. Being self-sufficient meant knowing when to admit you'd been wrong and taking the extra step of apologizing.

Reaching for one of her favorite baking books, she flipped to the pie section. Up next on the plate was a huge apology to Jasper Dumont.

Jasper decided to take a risk. Two risks, actually. The first was going over to Carissa's house to begin with. The second came to him as he drove by the local pizzeria en route to her aunt's cottage. He promptly pulled a U-turn and swung back around to it. Twenty minutes later he was back on course.

When she opened the door, a surprised look crossed her face and her mouth opened into an appealing little O. "Jasper, I can't believe you're standing there. How crazy."

Intrigued with her response, he said, "Crazy good or crazy bad?"

She considered. "Crazy, crazy. I have something for you. In fact, I was just on my way to come see you."

She tugged on an apron she was wearing. Under it was a pair of comfy-looking gray pants and a turquoise T-shirt that clung to all the right places. The outfit should have been frumpy, but with her body, the sweats were as good as wearing a black-tie gown. Her hair was piled on top of her head and there was a smear of flour on one cheek. His fingers itched to reach out and brush it away.

Instead, he produced the large pizza box from behind his back. The smell of the cheese and tomato sauce had his mouth watering on the drive over. He saw interest piqued in her eyes as she took in the pizza.

"I have something for you, too. I hope you still like your pizza the same way. Extra cheese and anchovies?" he asked.

The corners of her mouth twitched until she relented and let the smile blossom. "Still my favorite." She pointed a finger. "And the best topping of all time ever for pizza."

"So you always said. Can I come in?"

She stepped back. "What kind of idiot doesn't let a pizza in the front door?"

"Good point."

He took in the cottage as they made their way back to the kitchen. He chuckled. "I haven't been in this house in ages." He picked up a small clock nestled inside a large seashell that was bedecked with glitter and shook his head. "Same old Val."

She grinned. "It's comforting, really. She hung wallpaper in the bathroom. Peach wallpaper with flowers. Also, I think she may be growing weed in the backyard."

"No kidding?" He stopped, tilted his head up, his nose twitching. "What's that smell?"

She smiled. "It's your surprise." Moving to the left, she

revealed the source of the aroma. "I made a peach pie for you."

He grinned and pumped his fist in the air. "My favorite. But what's the occasion?"

"What was the occasion for the pizza?" She nodded at the box.

"You first," he said.

Her smile faded. "An apology. I'm so sorry for accusing you of outing me to the Bayside Blogger. Things have been so tough this year and coming back here and…"

She trailed off when he raised a hand. "You don't have to go into all of that, Car."

She removed her apron. "I hurt your feelings."

"You did," he admitted easily.

"I'm sorry."

"I accept."

She cocked her head. "Just like that?"

He nodded. "Just like that."

She threw her apron onto the table. "You are infuriating. You're not even making me work for it."

"Not my style." He leaned over and wiped the streak of flour from her skin, allowing himself to linger there a moment longer than necessary. Then he met those intoxicating gray eyes. "I care about you, Car. I always have. I always will. Your being a bit angry for one night isn't going to change that. You'd been hurt, and I get it. Even if I didn't like bearing the brunt."

He'd thrown her off balance with that. He liked puzzling her. She got the cutest little line on her forehead when she tried to figure out something that baffled her.

"You're too sweet, Jasp," she finally said.

"Sweet?" He nabbed a piece of the piecrust and popped it into his mouth. "I'm other things, too."

"Yes, you are." She batted his fingers away from the pie. "Now your turn. What's with the pizza?"

He shrugged. "Just like that night in the bar, I thought you could use a friend."

"A friend, huh? Being my friend wouldn't have anything to do with a certain blogger's recent article about me?"

He opened his mouth but quickly shut it. He coughed. "I think we need to eat this pizza before it gets cold. Plus, the sooner we eat this, the sooner we can eat that." He pointed at the pie.

Carissa offered him a knowing smile but she didn't say anything. Instead, she went to a cabinet and came back with two plates and a stack of napkins. "How about we eat this out on the deck? It's a nice night."

While he brought the pizza and plates outside, she grabbed a bottle of wine and glasses. A few moments later she emerged with an uncorked bottle of red.

"This might be the best meal ever," she said after she took her first bite. Her eyes were closed and she made the most seductive sound he'd ever heard. Jasper's mouth watered yet again, only it had nothing to do with the pizza this time.

They ate in companionable silence for a while. But after Carissa finished her second piece, she took a long pull of wine and turned to him.

"I'm catering a bridal shower. Elsie Reynolds read the Bayside Blogger's column today and tried to fire me."

He felt his eyebrow rise. "Tried to?"

"I didn't let her."

Good girl. He put his plate down and faced her. "Was the article true?"

"You mean, is it true that I don't have any catering experience?" She was staring straight ahead at the water. "Yep, pretty much."

"Car, why didn't you tell me that? You know I would have helped you."

Her head whipped around and her eyes focused on his. "That's exactly why I didn't. I spent the last decade completely out of control, dependent on someone else. Finally, I have the opportunity to gain some independence, some freedom."

And she needed to do this for herself, he realized. Jasper got that. He'd been the same way when he'd finally started applying himself in college.

"She tried to fire you and you didn't let her. Looks like you are in business for yourself." He tapped his wineglass against hers and reveled in the smile that blossomed over her face. "Carissa," he began, but she jumped up suddenly, as if sensing the mood shift between them.

"I think it's time for pie."

He decided to give her a break. "I think it's always time for pie."

A few minutes later they were both finishing up their slices of what Jasper deemed the very best peach pie he'd ever had. And that included the Dumont chef's masterpiece.

"Elsie Reynolds is very lucky she kept you. Damn, that was good," he said, dropping his fork on the plate.

She laughed. "I'm glad you like it. The rest is yours to take home and eat in the middle of the night while standing in your kitchen naked."

"Who says I stand in my kitchen naked?"

"You don't?"

"Nope, if I'm eating pie naked, it's always in the living room."

Her grin lit up the deck, which was growing dark thanks to the diminishing sun. "Oh, sorry to have mixed that up," she finished on a laugh.

He smiled, enjoying the happiness of just being with

her. "Sometimes when we joke around like this, it feels like you never left."

She nodded, but once again she let her gaze slide toward the water. "I know what you mean. It feels so easy with you." She rose and walked toward the end of the deck. When she faced him again, her eyes were clouded, her face serious. "I need to tell you something, Jasp."

"Is it something that will end with more promises of pie?"

Her chest rose and fell as if she was silently laughing. "It's something that should end with the promise of a dozen more pies."

He crossed the deck, stood beside her. "Then, I'm definitely listening."

"This isn't the easiest thing for me to talk about, but I want to tell you why I broke up with you after graduation."

He hadn't been expecting that. Part of him had wanted to know the answer to this puzzle more than he wanted to breathe. But another part felt anxious about finally understanding the answer to something that had been a deep source of hurt for over a decade. Would learning the truth make him feel better or relive the hurt?

"Okay," he said tentatively.

She bit her lip and narrowed her eyes, as if she was trying to figure out where to start. He retrieved their wineglasses, pouring more while he waited. He didn't really want any more but he needed to do something.

Carissa accepted the wine. "You know…that is, my dad…well, my dad and I didn't have the best relationship."

"I remember." He took a sip. "I never really understood why, though. Your dad was fun. He always made me laugh."

"He always made everyone laugh." She pushed a hand through her hair. "He was the life of the party. Everyone loved him. He was witty and clever and charming."

"Yes, he was," Jasper said slowly, wondering where this was going.

"He was also unreliable."

Surprised by that statement, Jasper leaned against the deck and waited for her to continue.

"I remember being in elementary school, about eight or nine. We were having a career day where our parents came in and talked about their jobs."

"I remember that," he said.

"Do you remember that my dad didn't come in to speak to the class? He couldn't, because he had nothing to talk about. He had no career. It was the first time I remember feeling disappointed by one of my parents. No—" she shook her head "—that's not quite right. I was embarrassed. I told the class that my dad had gotten sick and couldn't make it in for career day."

Jasper opened his mouth to object but no words came out. As he thought back, he quickly realized that he didn't know what either of Carissa's parents had done for work.

She laughed but the sound was metallic and humorless. "You're trying to think of what my parents did and you can't, right? Occasionally my dad would get into business with someone. Usually one of his friends. But it would never last. I honestly think he enjoyed the social aspect of working more than the actual work. Nothing ever stuck. He never had any ambition or desire to better himself.

"You're probably wondering how we lived in that big house on the water," she continued. "They lived off my mom's trust fund. A rather large trust fund from my grandparents. But even large amounts of money can be mismanaged. That brings me to you."

When her eyes met his, Jasper saw pain and anger there. Maybe some unresolved feelings, too.

"One morning after graduation, my parents sat me down

and explained that they'd run out of money. Just like that. It was all gone. Sometime during our senior year, my dad attempted one last-ditch effort with some business venture. He used the money set aside for my education. The venture never took off, just like all the others. And because of that, I had no way to pay for college."

His stomach tensed. "Oh, Car. I had no idea."

She nodded. "No one did. If I thought the humiliation of elementary career day was bad, it was nothing compared to that morning. I'd gotten into Northwestern and I'd been so excited to go there."

"But you did go there. Didn't you?" he asked.

"Yes, I did. Aunt Val helped me apply for scholarships, grants, you name it. She bought all the books and supplies I needed for the first year, too. I worked a lot during those four years. When I got married, Preston absorbed a ton of debt. For my twenty-fifth birthday he wrote a check and cleared out my loans." She snapped her fingers. "Just like that. Debt gone. Memories erased."

"But it's not that easy," Jasper said.

"No, it's not. In a strange way, the experience was good for me. I'd been a spoiled, pampered kid. I don't regret having to work hard. What I have a hard time with is my parents, particularly my dad. It felt like he had no concept of how much his actions affected others. In that case, me. Plus, they explained that they would be moving away from Bayside. They didn't want their friends to find out that they had nothing. They live in Maine now. So on top of everything else, I was losing the only home I'd ever known."

"You used to say that you hated it here and couldn't wait to get out," he reminded her.

"Oh, Jasp, I was just a kid. I didn't know what I was saying. I was a bratty girl who dreamed of the stars. And then one morning, I realized just how far away those stars were going to stay."

Jasper never imagined that she'd gone through so much with her parents. He was trying to absorb everything but it was a lot to think about. Then she threw one more bomb his way.

"I've told you that you always reminded me of my dad. I think that when all of that happened, I took it out on you. I mean, I didn't mean to do that. Not consciously anyway."

He held up a hand. She looked so young, so vulnerable. "Your dad had just hurt you and stripped away everything you had known and were counting on. You saw similarities between me and your father. So you broke up with me."

He was struggling. On the one hand, he wanted to be understanding. Carissa was opening up to him. At the same time, just talking about this was bringing up all that hurt and all that angst; as if a hand had reached into his chest and started squeezing his heart.

Her eyes welled up with tears. But he watched her take a few breaths and push those tears back down.

"When the first big betrayal of your life comes from one of your parents, it really messes with you," she said quietly.

He reached for her hand and was happy that she let him hold it. "I'm sorry, Car. Sorry you had to go through all that. I wish you would have told me back then. You know my family would have helped you."

She squeezed his fingers. "I was too mortified. I felt so ashamed. And scared."

"Where do things stand now with your parents?"

She shrugged. "Not great. I barely speak to my dad. My mom and I are okay. I guess."

"You guess?"

"I check in with her. But to be honest, I will never understand her. Why did she stay with my dad? He wasted all of her money. He had no ambition. They still live together, as if everything is fine. He didn't take care of her. Or me."

Her voice hitched on that last word. Jasper saw the emotion flooding her face.

"I was the good child. I never questioned anything. And then I got married to someone I thought I loved. I thought Preston adored me. I thought he was the opposite of my father. I thought he would do anything for me. Maybe he would have. But in the end, it didn't matter. He didn't love me, either."

And that was the heart of the mystery that was Carissa Blackwell. Jasper felt like his eyes had just been opened after a very long time of staying firmly shut. Carissa was this amazing, beautiful, smart woman with an abundance of confidence on the outside. But underneath it all, she was hurting. Her trust and her heart had been betrayed. She just wanted to be loved. That was all.

And he understood perfectly. Because under all of his flirting and bravado, Jasper craved the same thing. Love.

He ached for her. For that little girl in elementary school, for the teenager who almost had her life taken away, for the wife who'd been cheated on.

She pointed at him. "Don't do that."

"What?"

"Don't feel sorry for me. I am the one who was awful to you. I'm sorry for the way I broke up with you. I'm so sorry if I caused you any pain."

He let out a frustrated sound. "Of course you caused me pain. I loved you, you broke up with me out of the blue, and I was confused. But given everything you've said tonight, I can't help but feel for you. Not pity. I just feel *for* you."

And he did. More than that, he was suddenly seeing Carissa in a whole new light.

* * *

Carissa didn't know what to think or how to feel. She'd revealed her deepest, darkest, dirtiest secret.

She'd expected to still feel that shame, that discomfort. Surprisingly, she actually felt lighter, freer.

"I hadn't planned on spending the evening this way, but I'm really glad I told you all of this," she confessed.

He smiled. "I'm glad you told me, too. I wish I had known sooner, but I understand completely."

His eyes were so mesmerizing. She could stare at them for days at a time. The blue color was so brilliant and welcoming. When she talked to Jasper, it was as if she was the only person on the planet. More than that, it was like whatever she was talking about, big or little, was the most important thing in the universe. No wonder everyone wanted to be around him. Be with him.

She remembered something. "Um, should I ask you whatever happened to that girl from the other night? The woman you had the date with before you found me on the side of the road," she supplied.

Finally, he drank his wine. A rather large sip, she noticed. "I think you have a pretty good idea how that ended."

She raised an eyebrow in question.

"The date wasn't that great."

Yikes. "Sorry," she said.

"Are you?" he asked.

"Not really." She let out a harsh, bitter laugh. Carissa couldn't believe she'd just admitted that. "It's wrong, I know. I shouldn't wish your dating life any ill will. But I do."

His smile faded. A breeze came off the water. She'd let her hair down and she could feel the long blond strands blowing around her face. Something shifted between them. He put the wineglass down and closed the distance between them. "It's wrong. For so many reasons. But since you got back, I feel drawn to you."

She'd experienced the same sensation and yet his words had the breath leaving her body. "We've kissed a couple times."

"Yes, we have."

"I will blame the first one on alcohol. And fried cheese sticks."

"I don't get how the cheese sticks factor in but I'll agree." He tilted his head. "What about the second time?"

"Imminent danger always ups your adrenaline."

"We're now calling your overheated car imminent danger?" he asked.

"As long as you buy that."

"The kisses probably shouldn't happen again," he said, running his hands up her arms.

Her tongue darted out to wet her lips. "You're right. Definitely no more kissing."

And that's when he kissed her. His mouth met hers in a slow, sensual buildup that left her breathless. She wound her arms around his neck as he pulled her closer.

This was no ordinary kiss. This was the kiss of old-school Hollywood movies. It was like that one where… And then she couldn't think anymore. Not about movies or kisses or anything except Jasper Dumont.

After a very long time of devouring her mouth, he pulled back, running his thumbs over her cheeks and using those baby blues to dazzle her erratically beating heart even more.

"I told Riley and Elle that you were an amazing kisser," she said, her voice breathless.

Interest at this statement shone in his eyes. "Really? You talk about me with Riley and Elle?"

"Oh yeah. Girls talk about everything."

He pushed against her and she realized that he was just as aroused as she was. "Everything?"

She bit her lip. "Well, almost everything."

He grinned. "Then, let's give them something to really discuss next time you're together."

"What did you have in mind?"

He leaned in and nuzzled the side of her neck. "How about some of this?" He sucked her earlobe into his mouth, sending shivers down her spine.

"Yeah, that's, uh, good." He was scrambling her thoughts again. Any hope of stopping this evaporated.

"Maybe some of this," he said as his hand made its way up her side, grazing her breast.

Then she realized there was no reason to stop this. Why end something that felt so right?

"We could try some of this, too." She moved his hand so that it firmly settled over her breast.

"What a great idea. You are very wise." He cupped her breast, rubbing his thumb over her straining nipple.

Her head fell back as a moan sounded. "Jasp, maybe we should move this inside?"

"Why?" He kissed her again. "You have this nice big lot, protected by trees on either side and that fence over there."

"Jasp, we can't." But even as she said it, she was reaching for the waistband of his pants. She ran her fingers along his skin there, enjoying the way he sucked in a breath.

"When did you lose your sense of adventure? Remember that time on the football field?" He winked before he returned to her neck, sending delightful tremors down her spine. "I think Chicago took that bold, fearless girl away."

He was goading her and she knew it. Still, she fell for it. "Oh yeah?" With one fell swoop, she had his pants undone and yanked his shirt up and over his head.

"Impressive," he said on a strangled laugh.

So was he. Damn, she thought. Jasper was all grown up. The tall, lanky boy had definitely filled out. He was still in excellent shape but there was just more of him now. Just to make sure he was real and not some fictional daydream, she ran her hands over his chest, his broad shoulders, down his lean torso. She smiled when he jumped. "Still ticklish, I see."

"Shh, that's our secret."

"Yeah, mine and all the other women you've been with." Until the words escaped, she hadn't realized how much that thought bothered her. She frowned.

"Hey." He tilted her head up with one long finger. "You're the only one here with me now. Only you. The most beautiful woman I've ever seen." He kissed her deeply.

He still made her feel special. Even after everything she'd told him tonight. She stepped back and removed her shirt and then her lacy blue bra. His appreciative look made her feel feminine and powerful.

Before she could blink, he'd come to her and was everywhere. His fingers, his lips, his tongue. He ravished every part of her he could reach. When his mouth settled over her breast, she wound her fingers into his hair and hung on for dear life, even as the sensations threatened to break her.

After some time of being feasted on, she reached into his boxer briefs and cupped him. He groaned and then pressed his mouth to hers again. Slowly, she moved her hand over his length, listening to his accelerated breathing.

"Car, I…we need to…"

She got the message. Removing her hand, she pushed the briefs all the way off. He quickly reached down for his pants and removed a small foil packet. After that was taken care of, she plastered herself to him again.

They continued kissing and touching as they headed toward a lounge chair. In the process, they finished shedding all of their clothing.

She pushed him back and quickly straddled him. Rising above him, she took a moment to enjoy the look of pure lust in his eyes. She could only imagine that her own face would mirror the same expression of desire.

With another long kiss, she lifted her hips and took him in. They let out matching moans as she adjusted to the feel and size of him. Then he gripped her hips, urging her to move but accepting that she would set the pace. All while never taking his eyes off hers.

The moment was massively erotic. Being outside, with the wind cooling off their overheated skin, the sounds of the water lapping against the beach and the fading sunset illuminating their joined bodies, Carissa had never felt so turned on.

She began to move, slowly at first. But it wasn't long before she started needing more and more. Jasper complied by pumping his hips up to meet her beat for beat. Before she knew it, she was rising higher and higher, her moans and gasps mixing with Jasper's. She felt him tensing just as she fell off the cliff of desire. And he joined her right after.

Sated, she collapsed onto him. His arms circled her body protectively. Turning her head, she brushed a kiss over his mouth. Overwhelmed with his generosity throughout the whole night, she could think of nothing to say but "thank you."

He answered by staring deeply into her eyes for a long time. Then he kissed her and they finally rested. No more words needed.

Chapter Nine

Carissa woke first. As the sun streamed into her bedroom, she took a moment to gather her thoughts and take inventory of her body.

She quickly found that she felt amazing. Sated and content, she wanted to stretch her arms high over her head and purr like a cat. But the masculine arm draped over her side stopped her.

Slowly, she shifted so she could take in Jasper. Even in sleep, he wore a tranquil smile. His blond hair was mussed, stubble shadowed his jaw, and the sheet had draped low so his full chest with its smattering of appealing hair lay bare. In other words, he looked like sin on a stick, she thought, stifling a giggle.

He'd been amazing last night, and she wasn't even thinking about his moves in bed. Although those were quite improved from high school, and that was saying something.

Coming over here to check on her, when really, it should have been her to reach out to him. Then he'd listened so intently, without judgment, to her story.

Excluding Aunt Val, it had been the first time she'd ever

fully shared her thoughts on her parents. This morning, she had that amazing sensation of the proverbial weight being lifted from her shoulders.

He mumbled something in his sleep and that too made her smile. She wanted to do something nice for him so she quietly slipped from the bed. After a quick stop in the bathroom to freshen up—and okay, put on a quick coat of lip gloss—she entered the kitchen and started a pot of coffee.

As she waited for it to brew, she decided she was buying Aunt Val a Keurig for Christmas. But since she had a minute, she peeled an orange, arranging it on a plate. When the coffee was ready, she added mugs and the general coffee accessories to a tray and made her way back to the bedroom.

When she entered, she was greeted by Jasper's full-wattage smile. "Good morning, gorgeous," he called from the bed.

"Good morning to you."

"I thought maybe you were ashamed of me and ran out in an embarrassed huff."

She brought the tray to the bed. "I considered it. But in the end, I thought caffeine was a better and more mature option."

She handed him a mug and took her own. His eyes closed in contentment at his first sip. "This is from The Brewside," he said with certainty.

"You were right about their coffee. I'm quite addicted already."

They enjoyed the coffee and orange. Carissa ran to the door and grabbed the newspaper, which they read together in bed. It was all very comfortable and normal, until the hairs on the back of her neck stood up. Over the rim of her mug, she saw that he was watching her intently. Only, he wore an expression that she couldn't quite identify on his handsome face.

"What are you thinking?" she wondered aloud.

Without hesitation he said, "I was just thinking about how we've never done this before." He patted the bed.

She could feel her eyes widening in surprise. He'd clearly lost his mind. "Um, Jasp, we've kinda done *this*," she said, pointing toward the bed, "many, many times."

He shook his head. "I know we've slept together. I only meant we've never *slept* together. You know, woken up in each other's arms before." He ran a hand over her cheek. "I've never seen you first thing in the morning."

That statement shocked her into silence. My God, he was right. They'd been horny, hormone-driven teenagers. They'd hooked up all over Bayside in every sense of the term *hook up*. But of course, at the end of every night, they'd had to return to their respective houses.

The idea of making love, falling asleep in each other's arms, only to wake together as well, had simply never been in the cards.

This morning had been a first. A first that clearly meant the world to Jasper, if the way he was looking at her now meant anything. And it meant the world to her, too, only she found it hard to say that out loud. So she did something else.

First she placed her mug on the nightstand and then Jasper's. She pushed the newspaper off the bed and took complete advantage of his mouth. The morning make-out session was better than the coffee at waking her up.

After a long round of kissing and caressing, Jasper said, "Spend time with me."

She wiggled her hips and ran her leg up and down his. "I kinda think we're spending some time together right now."

He kissed her nose and trailed his hand up and down her arm. "And I like this kind of time. Trust me. I love it. But I was thinking about something else."

"Oh yeah?"

"Spend the day with me," he whispered against her mouth.

"I don't know, Jasp."

"Afraid people will talk about you?"

She rolled her eyes. "Not anymore. People are already talking about me. I was thinking that I should go over some recipes and think about my events for the next week. Try to drum up more business."

"There's this thing called a weekend. People who work usually enjoy them. Even CEOs. Trust me, I know."

She gazed into his eyes, realizing her mistake a moment too late. There was no way she could say no now. That blue gaze was a potent weapon.

"Fine," she relented. "I'll spend the day with you." She started untangling herself from him, but Jasper pulled her back and flipped her so he was towering over her. "What are you doing?" she asked.

"I forgot to tell you. Our day together starts right here in this bed."

She reached down and felt exactly how ready he was for the day. She grinned. "What a start."

True to Jasper's word, they started the day in bed. And then in the shower.

Once they finally left the house, with a quick stop for Jasper to grab clean clothes at his loft, they made their way to a local restaurant near the bay. They sat outside and enjoyed a long and luxurious brunch with decadent Belgian waffles, fresh fruit and sinfully rich coffee.

Then Jasper led her to the bay and his sailboat. She couldn't miss the name of the boat. *Determination.*

Coming around the dock, he noticed she was staring at the name. "I, uh, bought this little thing right after college.

Spent a lot of time fixing it up myself. Took a lot of determination to get it in working order."

She had a feeling that wasn't the only meaning of *determination* in Jasper's life. Once again, she felt ashamed at the things she'd said to him back when she'd broken up with him. She suppressed the urge to grab his face in her hands and demand that he realize how sorry she was. Instead, Carissa offered an encouraging smile. "It's a good name."

The awkwardness didn't linger once they were out on the water. It had been some time since she'd been in a boat, with the wind in her hair, the salty crispness of the water around her. She loved tilting her face to the sun and feeling its warm rays shower down on her. There wouldn't be too many more days like this. In a couple weeks, the weather would start to cool off, the leaves would begin to change colors, and summer would be nothing but a memory.

But for right now, she was enjoying watching Jasper in his element. After a couple hours, he pulled up to an older part of town. As she'd said to Jasper previously, there really weren't seedy parts of Bayside. However, this definitely wasn't a spot to send the tourists.

A large structure sat right on the water. She noticed a couple signs. Looked like a clothing boutique and a liquor store, and the rest of the doors appeared to be out of business.

Hand in hand, they walked up the dock.

"What is this place? Doesn't look too good," she said.

"Dumont Incorporated actually owns this property."

Surprised, she eyed him. "I'm shocked that you would allow such disrepair in the Dumont portfolio."

He laughed. "One step at a time. We've had a lot of offers on this place. The most persistent one from an adult entertainment store."

"A what?"

"You know, a place that sells videos and toys. Plus, you can get racy lingerie and, ahem, accessories for active adults." He accented the word *accessories*.

Whoa. "By active, I'm assuming you don't mean hiking and running."

He chuckled. "More like active in bed."

Ah, she got it now. She scrunched up her nose. "I'm not judging. To each their own. Isn't there a place like that out on the highway, right before the exit ramp?"

Jasper nodded. "There used to be. It closed not long after you left. That's the thing. The closest adult store is fifty miles from here. There's a market."

"How does the town feel about that?"

"I'm sure some of them are ecstatic on the inside. But in public, not that happy, as you can imagine. I'll admit, their bid is high. A lot higher than the others, in fact."

She meant what she'd said to Jasper. She truly wasn't judging. Besides, Carissa wasn't an idiot. Plenty of people frequented that kind of establishment.

Jasper continued. "Should I sell to one person? Should I renovate and then lease out space again? There's another possible idea, but it's out of the norm and therefore might not sit well with the board."

He looked tired just talking about it, like it was something that had been keeping him up at night. She touched his arm. "This is important to you."

"All of the deals are, but this one…let's just say that I want to make my mark with this one."

She got it. He wanted to show that he was the right man for the job. Despite his outward confidence, he was feeling insecure about heading up the family business. Carissa couldn't imagine how much pressure came with his job.

"In any case, whatever I decide to do here, it definitely needs a makeover on the outside, that's for sure. But I've heard my mom and Elle talk about this clothing boutique. I know they both do a ton of shopping here. Despite appearances, word of mouth has done wonders for this place."

"Elle does have fabulous taste in clothes, so maybe I should just peruse a little." She'd already untangled their fingers and was heading toward the door. She heard his laugh as she walked inside.

When she entered the store she was greeted by a pretty woman wearing a darling maxi dress in a fun, frisky chartreuse color.

"Welcome to Victoria's Attic. Can I help you find something today?"

"Just browsing. I've never been in here before. Are you Victoria?"

The woman smiled. "No, Victoria is the owner. I'm Leslie, the manager."

"Nice to meet you." Carissa shook her hand and they kept chatting as Carissa scanned the merchandise. There was an impressive array of flirty dresses, fabulous skirts, interesting tops and killer accessories.

She learned that Victoria, the owner, didn't come into the store much anymore. Instead, she let Leslie handle the day-to-day work.

"So you're a caterer?" Leslie asked with interest in her eyes.

"Trying to be. I'm just getting my business off the ground."

"I may be able to help with that."

Carissa dropped the silky lavender scarf she was coveting and gave Leslie her full attention.

"We hold a monthly ladies' night in the store. Nothing fancy. But everything is on sale. We have raffles and some other little games. I've been making most of the food myself. And by making it myself, I really mean that I beg every person I know to lend a hand. I'm surprised I have any friends left," she said with a wink.

"And you'd like to hire me to cater one of the ladies' nights?"

Leslie let out a relieved sigh. "Actually, I'd like to hire you to cater all of them."

"But you haven't even tasted my food or heard about what I can do," Carissa said.

"Actually, I was at the Dumont party and my best friend was at Mrs. Dumont's fund-raiser you catered. Trust me, we're both big fans already. Our ladies' nights are nothing fancy. Nothing like a Dumont party. Just appetizers and desserts."

Carissa couldn't believe her luck. Before Jasper had commandeered her weekend—and she meant that in a really good way—she'd planned on spending her time searching for more business to keep her new company afloat. Who would have thought a day of sailing would end up drumming up new business anyway?

She chatted with Leslie for a few more minutes, agreeing to send some menu options over later in the week. And because she simply couldn't resist, she bought the scarf, too. Refraining from doing a leap out the door, she clamped down on her excitement as she left the store.

But once she was outside, she practically bounced down the steps to where Jasper was standing, scrolling through his phone and waiting patiently for her. "Look at that smile."

She launched herself into his arms and hugged tight. "I'm amazing," she announced.

He leaned back and pushed a strand of her hair over her shoulder. "Yes, you are. Any particular reason why you've realized it recently?"

"Yes, I..." She trailed off when Jasper's phone began ringing. "Do you need to get that?"

He checked the display and nodded. "Just one sec. This is business."

"I thought CEOs didn't work on weekends," she called after him with a smile as he took the call and stuck his tongue out at her. When he returned, he seemed a little miffed. "What's up?" she asked, nodding toward the phone he was tucking back into his pocket.

"That adult entertainment shop again. They increased their bid. If they keep this up, it will be hard to keep the board from pressuring me to accept."

"You don't want to accept?" she asked.

"Let's just say that it would be very good business for us. But I have other plans for the space. However, if I do what the board wants on this one, I will make a lot of people very happy." He shook his head and grabbed her hand. "But enough of that. Are you hungry?"

"A little."

"Great, because I happen to know of a very romantic place with the best lobster you've ever tasted."

It was amazing how fast he could go between business and pleasure. She was fascinated watching him. On the one hand, he'd changed so much since high school. He was wheeling and dealing, running a huge and very successful business. Of course, he was still the same Jasper at heart. Still caring, still kind, still funny, and still the most handsome man she'd ever seen.

So engrossed with thoughts of him, she followed him back to the boat, her own business deal forgotten for the moment. He spoke of Dumont Incorporated a little more over dinner. Anyone could hear the pride he had in the company. But the business talk didn't last long. He quickly shifted into more casual conversation.

"So how do you like the lobster?" he asked.

Glancing around the hole-in-the-wall restaurant that sat

on the water a couple of towns over from Bayside, Carissa couldn't help but be enchanted. Small rickety tables were dressed up with old drippy candles, and twinkly lights were strung around the small patio where they sat. Stars twinkled overhead and soft music played out of speakers mounted on the walls. The smell of fresh fish wafted out of the kitchen.

She threw her napkin on the table. "You were right. This is definitely the best lobster I've ever had." And she really liked that she was having it in this small mom-and-pop restaurant rather than the fancy places Preston used to drag her to. He'd always claimed that he was a foodie, willing to try anything. In reality, he'd try whatever new restaurant opened up on Michigan Avenue. In her opinion, places like this were the real treasures of American cuisine.

"Say that again," Jasper said, reaching for her hand and entwining their fingers again.

"This lobster is amazing? I'll be saying that until my dying day."

He offered her a mischievous grin. "No, not that part. The bit where you said I was right."

She laughed and rolled her eyes at the same time. "Oh please. Such an ego on you."

"But I *was* right." He started playing footsie with her under the table.

She ignored his statement. Instead, she moved her foot far up his leg, delighting when he jumped.

"Are you trying to seduce me, Ms. Blackwell?"

"Do I need to try?" she said cockily.

"Not even a little." He yanked her over the table and kissed her.

Even such a short, spontaneous kiss left her breathless. When they separated, she licked her lips, relishing the taste of him mixed with the lobster butter on his lips. "So what's next?" She fully expected him to make a quip about his bed or some other sexual thing. But he surprised her.

"I was thinking about dancing."

Besides some fun girls' nights back in college, Carissa had never been dancing. In fact, she didn't really know anyone who went dancing and had kind of doubted that it was even a thing. Instead, she thought it was some activity that writers made up to put in books and movies.

But here she was with Jasper, having one hell of a good time at a Latin club he knew about, having caipirinhas and salsa dancing. She had no idea Jasper even knew how to do this, but he sure did. She was so mesmerized by his gyrating hips that she kept stepping on his toes.

"I'm sorry," she said for the hundredth time, even as she laughed.

He pulled her closer. "You're overthinking it. Just follow my lead."

She would follow his hips to the end of the earth. But in the meantime, she'd settle for this dance floor. They kept it up for a couple hours. Finally, they both needed a break so they grabbed water from the bar and headed outside to a quiet spot.

"Are you cold?" he asked.

The temperature had dropped a bit from when they'd been out on the water earlier that day. "No way. This air feels great on my skin." They had matching layers of sweat from their dancing.

Carissa had to admit that she'd had more fun today than she'd had in a very long time. In fact, she couldn't remember the last time she'd let her hair down. From sailing to that amazing dinner to the dancing, everything had been perfect.

Jasper had been perfect.

Careful, she cautioned herself. Preston had been perfect, too. She didn't even realize she'd frowned until Jasper gently ran a hand across her forehead where she was sure a frown line had formed.

"Where did you just go?" he asked kindly.

"Back to Chicago," she answered without thinking. She really shouldn't bring this all up again. She turned from Jasper but he gently pulled her back.

"Tell me more," he said gently.

"I was thinking about my marriage."

"Anything specific?"

He was so damn patient. It made it impossible to keep anything from him. "I was thinking about how boring it was, actually." He seemed surprised at the admission. "I mean, on paper it was… Well, let's just say that Preston would have never salsa danced. In fact, he would have never even known this place existed or had the inclination to ever find it."

"Everyone's different," Jasper said evenly. "What kind of stuff was he into? What did you guys do together?"

Not much, and wasn't that depressing. "We'd go to events for his company. Everyone spoke in hushed tones and pretended to like each other."

"Fun," Jasper said drily.

"Yeah, a real riot. He liked art. I do, too, but I tend to go for the bolder, brighter, more eclectic stuff. Preston prefers whites, beiges, very modern, very streamlined. He got me this painting for one of my birthdays and it was, well, I'm thrilled he wanted it back in the divorce. It was a white canvas with three black dots. I mean, what the hell is that?"

He chuckled. "Maybe the dots represent something."

"Yeah, like the boredom that was my marriage. Like the apathy of my husband toward me."

"What do you mean, Car? How could anyone be apathetic around you?"

She smiled even though she felt like crying on the inside. "I think that Preston chose to date me because I looked good on the outside. Because I was the perfect package of what a trophy wife should look like. To be honest, I don't think he ever really knew a damn thing about me." She was on a roll now and couldn't stop the words coming out of her mouth even if she wanted. "He didn't know my favorite band or the fact that I really like beer. And he definitely didn't know that I like extra cheese and anchovies on my pizza." She touched Jasper's chest. "One time I told him that I liked anchovies and he said we couldn't ever have them in the condo because they were too salty and we should strive to maintain a low-sodium diet."

She ran a hand through her hair. "I didn't see you for over ten years and you remembered. You remember everything about me, don't you?"

Staying silent, Jasper nodded.

"One time I tried to talk to Preston about my dad. He listened. He said he was sorry. But he never mentioned it again. My dysfunctional family would mar our perfect image. And it made me less amazing."

He kissed her then, out of the blue. Deeply, tenderly. When he pulled back, he framed her face in his hands. "Didn't he ever tell you how beautiful you are?"

"No," she whispered.

"Didn't he tell you that you are the most amazing person?"

She shook her head.

"Didn't he thank God every single day for the mere fact of getting to be with you?"

Beyond moved by his words, a single tear fell from her eye.

"Because getting to be with you, Carissa Blackwell, is the biggest gift in the world. He should have realized what he had."

She sniffled and moved her hands so they lay around his. "You see me differently than everyone else."

"Lucky me." And then he kissed her again.

Overwhelmed, Carissa hugged him tightly. Then she pulled herself together, pushed back and smiled up at him. "I'm sorry. I don't really know where all of that came from."

A crease formed on Jasper's forehead. "You don't have to apologize for feeling things. Not with me anyway. I think you needed to get that off your chest. I think you've been through a bad time and you're healing. Keeping it all bottled up will never help you."

"You know what will help me?" she asked with a sparkle in her eye.

"For me to go to Chicago and beat the snot out of your ex-husband?"

She let out a little chuckle. "Well, actually, yes. But I was thinking since the airport is closed already we could go back inside and do more salsa dancing."

He kissed her, grabbed her hand, and together they returned to the dance floor.

Jasper had learned to salsa dance from a girlfriend back in college, but he'd never enjoyed it as much as he had tonight. Even though Carissa was not the world's greatest dancer, she did try. And watching her eyes lock onto his lower region was definitely a turn-on.

Who wouldn't be turned on by her, though? Well, apparently her husband. What an asshat, he thought. But it wasn't the first time he'd thought it. After what she'd shared tonight, Jasper was truly shocked. He was also saddened. To know that she'd been disappointed first by her father and then by her husband made his blood boil. Especially when he knew how amazing she was.

Growing up together, he'd always gravitated toward her. And not only because of her looks. Even before they'd dated, he'd call her up when he wanted to do something fun. She'd always been up to try something new. Kayaking, fishing, laser tag, you name it. So it was interesting to learn that her husband hadn't been on the daring side.

Although after everything he'd learned this weekend, he got why she'd married him. Her father had been unreliable, and even though Preston sounded dull as hell, at least he'd been consistent and dependable. Maybe a little too consistently boring, but still.

He returned his attention to his dancing partner, who was laughing and throwing her hair back and finally getting the hang of the dance. They weren't out on the dance floor for too long before the sensual movements and close proximity of their moving bodies started to remind him of another intimate act.

When the music slowed down and they were swaying together, he saw the same look in her eyes as he was feeling. "Do you want to get out of here?" he asked softly, lingering a moment to nip at her earlobe.

"You have no idea," she said back, trailing her hand just a little too low to be appropriate in public.

Jasper settled their bar tab and they made their way to his car and then back to Bayside. Driving was difficult, though, as Carissa was dancing her fingers up his thigh. At every stoplight, he'd lean over and take her mouth until some driver laid on their horn.

As they neared his condo, Carissa leaned toward her window. "I'm still surprised they put apartments in Bayside."

"They're condos, actually, and my company did them.

We're really trying to revitalize Bayside. It's not a very large building. I actually just made a deal with someone for more apartments, retail space—"

"Jasper, that's great and I totally want to hear all about it. But um, right now…" She nodded toward the condos and squeezed his leg. "I really want you to take me inside."

He looked down at her hand. He had to hold back a growl from escaping. "Yes, ma'am."

Jasper had never parked his car so fast. After they left the underground garage, Jasper punched in a code on a keypad to let them into the elevator, which was thankfully empty at this hour because he couldn't hold himself back from attacking her. She plastered herself to his strong body as his arms went around her and his lips feasted on hers.

He didn't even remember the elevator stopping or walking to his condo at the end of the hallway. But clearly they must have made it because the next thing he knew, the door to his condo was flung open, banging against the wall, as their mouths stayed fused together.

"Before I forget, I had so much fun today," she said, ripping her mouth from his. But the rise and fall of her full chest, along with the pure lust shining in her eyes, told him she wasn't in for a long conversation.

Suddenly, their hands were everywhere at once. He kicked the door shut and felt her fingers running along the waistband of his pants. He couldn't stop his intake of breath at the feel of her fingers grazing along the sensitive skin of his stomach.

The moonlight was streaming through the large picture window, shining on her thick hair. He ran his hands through her locks, which allowed him to angle her head just where he wanted it. He plunged his tongue inside her mouth. She met him kiss for kiss, nip for nip, touch for touch.

He took her mouth again as she tugged at his pants.

While the kiss started off as steamy as the thing she was doing with her fingers, it soon turned soft and lingering. When he was done feasting on her lips—although, he didn't think he would ever really be done—he trailed his lips down the long column of her throat. She gasped, wrapping her arms tightly around him. Ah, still responsive there.

She pulled his shirt and he helped by reaching his arms over his head. With his shirt removed, her gaze swept over the length of him and she let out an appreciative sound.

It dawned on him that they were barely inside his condo. But the way her hands were all over his chest, igniting the skin everywhere she touched, made it abundantly clear they weren't going to make it all the way back to his bedroom. "Couch?" he asked with a strangled voice.

"Sure," she said, nipping at his bottom lip. But then she pulled him toward her roughly. Jasper lost his balance and they both fell to the hard floor. Luckily, he broke her fall, landing on his back with Carissa plastered on top of him.

She didn't waste any time. Her mouth was greedy as it devoured every inch of skin she could reach. Jasper felt helpless in the best possible way. He simply ran his hands over her curvy body as she had her way with him. When she pushed back and removed both her lacy top and the equally lacy red bra she wore underneath, Jasper's mouth went dry.

Damn, how could she be even more beautiful now than when they were teenagers?

"You're—" he began to say, but stopped when she put a finger to his lips.

"Shhh. Don't talk. Just touch me. Touch me everywhere."

Jasper was fine taking orders. Especially sexy orders that came from a half-naked woman straddling him.

They continued kissing, touching, caressing each other as the light from the moon made its way to their spot on the floor. Somehow she managed to shuck out of her jeans. He took advantage of the time to remove his own pants and boxer briefs. When she turned back and saw that he was completely undressed, a slow, seductive smile spread over her face. A strand of hair fell over her eye and she pushed all of it back. Then she leaned down, positioning her body flush with his. The feel of skin on skin was beyond heady. She kissed him deeply, their tongues mingling.

Everything felt so damn good. She was moving her body over his, teasing him with a preview of what was about to happen. He could feel the warmth at her center, a reminder that he needed to take care of safety first.

Flinging his arm out to the side, he quickly located his pants. It took another minute to work his wallet out of the pocket and retrieve the condom he'd just replaced that morning.

"Thanks," she said.

"Of course." And then he took her lips again.

"Carissa," he moaned as he flipped their positions. Looking down at her, he almost chuckled. Jasper would have never guessed the weekend was going to be like this back on Friday afternoon. But what an amazing surprise.

She reached between his legs, wrapping her fingers around his length. The gesture made him buck up in surprise. She offered him a cocky smile. But he got the advantage back when he took her breast in his mouth, sucking and licking her swollen nipple. By the time he moved to the other breast, offering the same attention, Carissa was moaning. He knew neither of them could wait another minute longer.

Positioning himself between her legs, Jasper took one more long look at her before entering her, filling her completely. Matching gasps escaped their mouths and Jasper leaned forward to catch her moan. Her nails sank into his back and she brought her knees up, urging him to move.

Jasper tried to stay slow, tried to use long, languid thrusts. But it didn't take long for him to become intoxicated by the feel of her. Surrounded by her sweet scent, the soft touch of her skin and the sensation of her limbs firmly locked around him, he was helpless to do anything but give in.

He pushed them harder and higher. Their voices rose together as they both panted out their pleasure. Before long, he began to see stars. Jasper knew the moment she came and pressed his mouth to hers. With three final strokes, he joined her on the other side of ecstasy.

Jasper wasn't sure how long they lay there together, their limbs a tangled mass on the cold, unyielding floor. Their rough inhalations eventually died down and the room was filled with the contented sound of deep, heavy breathing.

When he knew he could move again, he began running his hands up and down her arms. She let out a pleased murmur. Opening her eyes, she met his stare with those penetrating gray eyes.

Jasper knew he could get lost in her eyes. Knew he could, and probably would, spend hours obsessing over this night. That's why he decided to keep it light.

"So welcome back to my place."

She laughed. "Nice to be here sober this time. Impressive entryway. Nice floor." She patted the wood.

"I'm glad I went with the hardwood. Of course, I didn't exactly have *this* in mind when I picked it. Had I known you'd show up again, I might've chosen a softer material."

"Maybe next time I can see the bedroom."

"Got hardwood in there, too."

She punched his shoulder and he leaned down for another long, sultry kiss. When he lifted his head, he noticed an expression on her face he'd never seen before. "What's going on in there?" he asked, tapping a finger against her head.

"You don't want to know."

"Probably not. But tell me anyway."

She bit her lip, stalling for time. When she finally spoke, she said, "I'm happy."

Her words did more to his ego than closing any business deal ever could. His eyebrow arched. "Really?"

"It's been a long time since I've said that. So thank you."

"Come on." He reared back onto his feet, grabbed her hands, and pulled her up.

"Jasp, what are you—"

He cut her off with a long kiss. When her body went soft, he scooped her up in his arms, satisfied at the sound of a very feminine sigh.

"I think it's time for a proper tour."

She cupped his cheek in a gesture that was sweet and somewhat out of character. "I'd like that. Hopefully the tour will start with the bedroom."

"Honey, it starts, stays and ends with the bedroom."

She laughed. "My kind of tour."

With that, he walked them into the bedroom, where they remained the rest of the night. All of those questions and insecurities staying outside the partially closed door. For now.

Chapter Ten

Time is flying, my friends. It's officially autumn, a time for bonfires, football games and candy corn. Apparently, it's also a time for new relationships, because Carissa Blackwell and Jasper Dumont have become inseparable. Just like old times. Hopefully, nothing can break them up again...

Carissa wasn't superstitious, but she was cautious. And realistic. So to say that her life had been perfect lately was definitely a bit overzealous. However, even she could admit that things had been going well.

September ended and she couldn't believe it was October already. Then again, she'd been so busy it wasn't that surprising.

She'd catered the bridal shower for Mrs. Reynolds's daughter to fantastic reviews. When she was asked to cater the wedding in January, Carissa thought she would weep. But she kept it together, stayed professional.

Despite the Bayside Blogger's continued references to her in her daily column, no one in Bayside seemed to care much. And she hadn't been questioned again on her references or experience. She was actually making a name for herself.

In the meantime, she'd picked up other jobs here and there, including her first ladies' night at Victoria's Attic. It had gone well and she already had a ton of ideas for the next one. She definitely put extra energy into that event since it was still her only repeat customer. That meant a lot to her.

Other than work, she'd been hanging with Elle and Riley. It was nice to have girlfriends to go to the movies with, have drinks, share laughs. She realized that friends were another thing she'd missed during her marriage. All of her "friends" had been Preston's, and even when they did hang out it was to attend charity events and fund-raisers. Also, just like Preston, they'd been dullsville.

And then there was the opposite of dullsville. There was Jasper. Talk about excitement and fun and spontaneity. She sat back on the porch steps where she was waiting for him. He'd called earlier to say he had a big surprise for her.

She bit her lip as she considered. Two weeks ago he'd taken her to a concert where they'd danced and sung along all night. Last week he'd surprised her with a really amazing bottle of red wine. She licked her lips just remembering it.

But he wasn't the only one with the surprises. She baked for him constantly. The way to a man's heart really was through his stomach. She'd even come up with a recipe where she used The Brewside's coffee in a decadent chocolate cookie. His response to that one had been orgasmic. Literally, she thought with a grin, remembering the end of that particular night. It was safe to say their relationship was going well.

Their relationship. She sucked in a quick breath of air. When had it become a relationship? Maybe somewhere between the passionate nights they spent together and all of the places they went together.

They had a standing date every morning at The Brewside. She had to admit she looked forward to that short time with him. They'd have coffee, share a goody from the bakery display and talk about what they each had planned for the day. Then he'd buy a beverage for his assistant and they'd both go on their way.

What a simple routine. Simple, but meaningful. And exactly like a relationship. Her stomach tensed as a wave of panic hit her in the gut.

She wasn't ready for a relationship. She'd only been divorced a matter of months. She needed to wait... Carissa let that thought trail off as she chewed on a fingernail. Preston sure hadn't waited for the ink to dry. Besides, it wasn't like there was some definite amount of time set in stone that one had to wait before embarking on a new relationship again.

Relationship. There was that word again. That word that evoked feelings of trust and hope and love. All emotions that could be taken away in a flash. Isn't that what happened with Preston? Wasn't that what had happened with her father?

It seemed like every time she opened her heart to a man it was crushed. Well, except for one man. In that case, she'd done the crushing. And what if this time around, Jasper broke her heart? Being disappointed by Preston was one thing. But she didn't know if she could bounce back from Jasper.

Speak of the devil. Jasper's car came to a stop at the end of the driveway just then. He hopped out and walked to her, looking like some kind of Greek god out for a late-afternoon stroll.

"Hey, gorgeous," he called.

She stood up and closed the distance between them. "Are we in a relationship?" she blurted.

Jasper worked hard to make sure his smile didn't fade. It wasn't the words that came out of her mouth that caused it to falter, but more the emotion behind her question. The way her face tensed up and her eyes narrowed.

He'd loved getting closer to Carissa since she'd returned to town. While there were so many familiar things he remembered from high school, they'd both grown up. For better or worse, they were different people, and learning all of the new Carissa quirks was fun and exciting, too.

But in all of that time of reconnecting, Jasper had not been oblivious to the fact that she had issues to work through. He tried to give her the space to do that. Today, he wasn't sure where this question had come from, so he proceeded with caution.

"Well," he began, "we seem to spend a lot of time together."

She nodded. "True, but not all the time. I mean, we each have our own friends."

He was bemused by her statement. "Of course we do. We have some friends in common, too."

"Well, yeah. But what else?"

He considered this for a moment. "We're sleeping together."

"But that doesn't always translate to a relationship," she said.

"Maybe not, but I don't sleep with more than one person at a time."

"Me neither. So…we're sleeping together and we hang out a lot and…" She trailed off, looking down at the ground.

"Carissa," Jasper said, using his index finger to guide her head back up so she would look him in the eyes. "We're in a relationship." Then he drew her to him and kissed the living daylights out of her.

When they came up for air, he had to take a moment to collect himself. He'd kissed this woman thousands of times over the years and yet each time felt like the first.

"Car, we don't have to be in a super-serious, heading-to-the-altar kind of relationship. But to answer your initial question, yes, we are in a relationship."

"I want to build my company," she said, her lips swollen from their kiss.

Jasper raised an amused eyebrow at this statement. "Who's stopping you? And anyway, I have something to show you that might help with that company."

It was her turn to raise her brow. "Oh really, is this my surprise?"

"Yep." He leaned over and kissed her again. "Want to take a ride?"

He started walking toward the car before she could say yes. Carissa reached for his hand and tugged him back to her. Then she pressed her lips to his, gently, reverently. The softness of the kiss hit him right in the gut.

"Not that I mind," he said when they were done. "But what was that for?"

"'Cause that's what people do when they're in a relationship." He couldn't stop a grin from spreading, and then she punched him in the arm. "But not a super-serious relationship."

He wisely changed the subject as they got in his car and drove away. "How's Aunt Val?"

"Great, as usual. She's in Spain now."

Jasper drove through the center of town and out toward the outskirts. "No doubt she's drinking too much sangria and causing all kinds of raucous trouble."

"No doubt," Carissa agreed.

They listened to the radio, both singing along to a song that was popular during their senior year of high school, until Jasper turned onto a tree-lined street.

"Oak Avenue," she said. "What are we doing here? You want to go shopping at Victoria's Attic?" She wiggled her eyebrows. "Because I wouldn't mind that."

"I think I'll leave the shopping to you." Jasper threw the car into Park and hopped out. Then he came to her side and opened her door. Carissa got out, gave another look at Victoria's Attic, and then arched her eyebrow in question.

"Spill. What's going on?"

His grin was fast and devastating. "I have made one of the best deals of my career." He made a sweeping arm gesture to include the building.

Carissa waited patiently. "More details, please. Because right now I'm looking at a big building."

"A big building that won't be here next month."

Jasper could barely contain his excitement. He'd been working day and night on this deal. There were a lot of moving parts, a lot of people this affected.

The board had been putting on the pressure for him to accept the adult entertainment shop, but it had felt wrong. When he first started dropping hints he was thinking of a bookstore, he'd gotten some expected pushback.

But he'd kept working on the proposal until the board had seen the benefit to Bayside. Jasper was offering multiple businesses and more jobs to the local economy than one racy shop. His plan housed a bookstore with both the latest publications and a nod to his favorite high school hangout with a robust used section. There would be an adjacent event space. And his favorite part, a café.

All day, he'd been dying to tell Carissa. A café would offer her steady employment, yet she could still do her catering jobs. She could set her own hours, hire an employee or two.

Carissa was taking in the building. "Wh…where's it going? Oh no, the sexy adult shop?"

"No lingerie. I'm tearing down the building," he said gleefully. "Gone, kaput, dust and rubble."

"What's going to happen to the businesses here? Victoria's Attic and that liquor store," she asked in a quiet voice.

"Gone."

"Are they moving somewhere else?"

That was an odd question. "Not that I know of. Victoria's Attic is closing permanently. See?" He pointed to a sign on the door.

Carissa walked closer to read it. Final Sale, Everything Must Go, Jasper read from where he stood.

She whirled back to Jasper. "They're closing?"

"Yep," he said proudly. "You are looking at the future home of the Bookworm."

She responded with a blank expression.

He grabbed her hands and squeezed. "Car, remember that old used bookstore we used to hang out at all the time in high school? I'm going to open one just like it."

"Sure. But what do you know about running a bookstore?"

He chuckled. "Not a lot. But I won't be running it. I'll find someone to do that. I know it's risky. But I think I can make this work. New and used books, access to online sites, rooms for students to meet and study, and a whole event space next door. Plus, the best part." He paused for dramatic effect. "A café that serves killer food."

He waited, holding his breath. But she didn't say anything. Didn't jump into his arms and kiss him. Didn't say thank you.

Jasper dropped his hands. "But first we need to do a massive renovation because the structure is a mess."

She remained silent, so he started rambling. "This idea met with some resistance at first, but now it's made everyone happy."

Stepping back, she aimed him with a level gaze. "Everyone?"

He wasn't sure what was going on in her head. "What's wrong, Car?"

Shaking her head, she stepped to him, placed a palm against his cheek and offered a small smile. "I'm happy for you, Jasp. This is an interesting idea and I definitely like it more than that adult shop." She scrunched up her nose.

"But?" he guessed.

"I don't mean to rain on your parade or make this about me, but I'm just a little disappointed."

Not what he'd been expecting her to say. "Babe, why?"

She glanced back at Victoria's Attic. "They're my only regular client. I know that's small potatoes compared to what you can do here."

Ah, he understood now. Plus, he hadn't told her the best part yet. "Your work is not small potatoes in any scenario. I had thought about the ladies' nights. I offered Victoria a lease on a different location. A better location, actually."

"You did?" She reached for his hands again, hope springing up in her eyes.

He nodded. "Turns out, she's ready to retire. I'm really sorry about that, Car."

"Well, you tried, at least. I'm sure I'll find other regulars."

His heart rate picked up at the opportunity. "I know you will. In fact, I might be able to help with that."

She smiled. "You're going to throw a party every Friday and hire me to cater it?" Her smile faded. "Actually, that sounds exactly like something you would do. I think that kind of investment might be more than my non-super-serious-relationship partner should have to endure on my behalf."

"I have a better idea. I want you to run the café." He gently turned her shoulders so she was staring at the building. "You would have total control. You pick the name, set the hours, the prices, everything. Plus, there's enough room to have a full working kitchen. You can run your catering business out of this location."

She spun back to him. "Are you serious, Jasp? Like really serious?"

He held his breath. "Yep."

Carissa was quiet for a long time as myriad emotions crossed her face. Her brain looked like it was running at full capacity. Finally, a huge grin lit up her face. "Jasper, ohmigod!"

She threw herself into his arms and kissed every inch of his face she could find. "Thank you, thank you, thank you. I won't let you down. Ohmigod," she repeated. "Would I really have full control?"

"Absolutely. I know even less about catering and cafés than I know about bookstores. And I know I said you could name it yourself, but I do have an idea."

She paused. "You do?"

"Make this an extension of your catering company. I know you wanted to add photos of some of your food on your website. This would be a real-life sample of what Save the Day Catering can do. The Save the Day Café," he finished, gesturing grandly at the building.

Her lips pursed as she considered. "You know, I actually like that. And while breakfast food is always appealing, Bayside already has The Brewside—"

"Exactly," Jasper interrupted. "That's why I was thinking you should stick to the lunchtime crowd. We don't have many lunch places."

"Well, that's something to think about."

His excitement grew. "And you could even get a van and make local deliveries. I know a great company that can help with that."

She held her hands up. "Whoa there, tiger. Let's just give me a second to take this all in."

He backed off. "Of course. Sorry. So," he said, offering her his best grin. "You're not mad that I took away your regular client?"

"I think you've more than made up for it." She kissed him soundly. "Now I have so many ideas in my head. Wow, my own café."

"Let's go grab dinner and celebrate," he said.

Jasper couldn't feel any happier. Finally, he'd come up with a business deal all on his own. Something different from his parents and an out-of-the-box concept for Dumont Incorporated that would be good for the bottom line and for Bayside.

Not to mention, he was able to help Carissa in the process. Show her that he was very different from the carefree, party-loving boy from high school. Proving that he'd worked his butt off all of these years.

He was good enough.

"There are so many decisions to make," Carissa said. "I can't wait to start making lists and coming up with ideas."

As they walked back to the car, he added, "I have a ton of suggestions for you. I've already called in some favors and lined up a couple meetings for you."

Jasper was so thrilled she'd gone for this idea that he missed her frown.

* * *

Carissa stared at her laptop, mouth hanging open, as she read over the Bayside Blogger's latest column.

Golden boy Jasper Dumont is opening a bookstore with a café. And who is going to be running this café, you ask? Shocker! His girlfriend, the recently returned Carissa Blackwell. Guess Carissa has moved from one man to another in record time. Not that I blame her. I'd love to be taken care of by Jasper Dumont, too…

She shut the lid of her laptop and pursed her lips. What did the Bayside Blogger mean by that?

She wasn't moving from one man to another. Although the ink had barely dried on her divorce papers and she was in a relationship with Jasper. And now they were going to be working together, too.

But she'd work her butt off to make this business succeed. In turn, Jasper would turn a good profit. Needing a pep talk, Carissa reminded herself that she had majored in business at Northwestern. And she was already well on her way to setting up her own catering company. She could do this. Jasper or no Jasper.

Besides, she had to admit she liked having a partner. Someone to bounce thoughts and ideas off. Of course, sometimes she did wish Jasper would tone it down a tad. As she was quickly learning, he could get a little too enthusiastic at times. Maybe that eagerness manifested in a bit of a controlling way, but the café was going to be hers. Jasper was only helping.

Then, why did she get a sinking feeling in the pit of her stomach every time she thought about it?

"You look like you're deep in thought," Elle said, breaking into Carissa's thoughts as she took a seat at the table in

The Brewside where Carissa currently had papers, note-books, her computer and two empty coffee cups spread out.

"Yes, no." Carissa shook her head. "It's nothing. Just a lot of details. What's going on?"

Elle looked great. She was wearing a light green dress that brought out her equally green eyes. Her brown hair was pulled back in a neat ponytail and her skin was glowing. Ah, to be in love.

"Taking a break from the gallery. I needed caffeine." Tony called out her name. "And there it is." Elle grabbed her drink and returned to the table. "What's all this?"

"Just ideas about the Save the Day Café. I'm meeting Jasper in a little bit to go over some things."

"I do love that name." Elle smiled.

"Me, too. Although it was actually Jasper's idea."

"You two have been working hard the last two weeks."

"What can I say? Jasper works fast. Demolition on the building happens next week."

"Wow, that is fast. How is it working with him?"

"Fine, I guess."

"You guess?"

Carissa couldn't stop her thoughts from returning to the last line of the Bayside Blogger's recent column. *I'd love to be taken care of by Jasper Dumont, too.*

That's not what this was. Right? It was a business arrangement. A business arrangement that he'd given to her without so much as a second thought. A business arrangement organized by her boyfriend.

She met Elle's curious gaze. There was a twinkle in her eye that was unmistakable. Why did people in love always want everyone else to be in love, too?

"What's with you today?" Carissa asked, ignoring Elle's original question. She pointed at her instead. "I can't put my finger on it but something is definitely different."

A coy grin spread across Elle's face. "I don't know what you're talking about." She touched her cheek. "I'm exactly the same as I was yesterday." She flipped her hand around.

"You are being so weird…" Carissa trailed off when the light caught the large diamond ring on Elle's finger. As soon as Carissa realized what she was looking at, Elle's smile became even brighter. If that was possible.

"Ohmigod, Elle." Even Carissa could hear the fluttery tone of her voice. "You're engaged!"

"Cam proposed last night." Elle's dimples winked as she thrust her hand forward. Carissa got a better look at the round diamond flanked by two pear-shaped emeralds set in what appeared to be a vintage band.

"This is gorgeous," Carissa squealed.

Elle studied the ring herself. "Cam said the emeralds reminded him of my eyes."

Carissa's heart gave a little flutter. "Did you have any idea?"

"None." Elle sat back. "I mean, we'd sort of danced around the topic. We spent the weekend at his cabin. We'd just finished dinner and were watching the sun set over the lake. I didn't even realize it, but next thing I know, he's down on one knee."

"Oh, Elle, I'm so happy for you guys." And she was. Elle and Cam were the perfect couple in Carissa's opinion. After their initial rocky reunion, Carissa and Cam had spent some quality time together, thanks to Jasper and Elle. She realized Cam only wanted the best for his little brother.

"It was so romantic. He asked my dad and everything. We told his parents this morning."

"I bet Mrs. Dumont was beside herself with happiness."

Elle laughed. "I think she already has the entire wedding planned. Plus, I heard her mention grandchildren as we were leaving. So watch out."

Carissa tilted her head. "For what?"

Elle extended a finger in Carissa's direction. "You're next."

"Next for…" Oh. She finally caught on to Elle's meaning. "I just got divorced, Elle. I have no plans to remarry in the immediate future."

Elle waved a hand. "I know that. But you and Jasper are really moving forward with gusto." She indicated all the papers on the table. "You're even working together."

Carissa's pulse picked up. "We're not working together exactly. I mean, I guess we are in the beginning phase."

"Who would have imagined all of this when you returned to Bayside?"

"Right." Her palms were sweating. She wiped them on her jeans. Who would have thought that when she returned to Bayside seeking her independence she would have jumped right back into a relationship with her high school boyfriend and accepted a job from him?

"You okay, Car?" Elle's eyes held worry.

Carissa felt horrible. This was Elle's day. She didn't need to steal her thunder with the dark thoughts circulating in her head. She forced a smile. A smile she really didn't feel on the inside.

"I'm fine. Just tired. And blissfully happy for you. We should celebrate."

"I haven't told Riley yet, so no celebrations until I do. And mum's the word."

Carissa pretended to lock her lips and Elle giggled.

"I have to get back to the gallery. But I'm glad I ran into you. Cam's telling Jasper the news now so next time you see him, tell him he'll make a lovely flower girl in the wedding."

Despite the anxiety Carissa was suddenly feeling, she smiled. "Will do."

An hour later, Carissa was seated in the waiting room outside Jasper's office. His assistant, Sherry, made sure she had a bottle of water.

"He'll just be about five minutes longer. The conference call he's on ran late," Sherry said.

"No problem. I'll just play around on my phone." Carissa grabbed her cell out of her purse.

She scanned through her emails but she wasn't really giving them her undivided attention. Instead, she couldn't stop thinking about, well, everything. Elle engaged, Jasper, the café, her independence, moving to Bayside, Mrs. Dumont wanting grandkids, her ex. Everything was a huge jumble.

As she clicked from email to email, she wound up on the Bayside Blogger's site again. "Damn gossip," Carissa said under her breath.

"What was that?" Sherry asked.

"Nothing. Sorry."

Embarrassed, Carissa glued her eyes to the screen as she perused another article. No mention of Elle and Cam's engagement yet. That was good news.

There was an item about Tony from The Brewside. Apparently, he'd gone on a date last night. Carissa kept scanning until she froze. Two mentions in one day. New record. She refrained from rolling her eyes and read the item instead.

Remember when the Dumont caterer ran out of the end-of-summer party last month? Carissa Blackwell helpfully stepped in, beginning her new career as Bayside's favorite caterer. And we've all enjoyed her culinary masterpieces since. Well, I've just learned that it was no coincidence. Jasper Dumont may have had a hand in getting his high school love the gig...

Carissa stared at the screen. She had no idea what to say or even how to feel at this new development.

How did Jasper have a hand in that night? Jasper was a good guy. Maybe the best she knew. But to set up that opportunity for her, well, it did reek of control.

Carissa searched her memory. The caterer had had a family emergency that night. How in the world could Jasper have orchestrated that? It was impossible.

Only nothing was impossible for a Dumont.

If the Blogger was right and Jasper meddled in her business then everything she'd been working so hard for hadn't been her own doing. She hadn't shaped her future. Jasper had. For the second time today, her palms began to sweat.

"Carissa," Sherry called. "Mr. Dumont will see you now."

With a heavy heart, Carissa rose and walked into Jasper's office.

Jasper loosened his tie. He'd already shed his jacket. He'd been looking forward to this meeting with Carissa all day. Before he could get to it, he'd been bombarded with meetings and conference calls. And one very happy lunch with his brother.

Carissa walked in looking sinfully amazing in tight jeans, a red blouse and a black blazer. Her hair was pulled back, revealing her long neck and accentuating her big gray eyes.

He crossed to her. "Hey, babe. Have you heard the news yet?"

She glanced down at the phone she was holding in a death grip. "Uh, yeah."

"Isn't it awesome?"

She met his eyes with confusion. "Awesome?" Then her face quickly changed, softened. "Oh, do you mean the news about your future sister-in-law?" Her normal smile finally surfaced.

"I had no idea Cam was planning that. He kept it under lock and key."

"Are you happy?"

He was beyond ecstatic. It had been a big year for his brother and seeing him with Elle left no doubt that he'd found his soul mate. "More than I can say. Words are inadequate."

"I'm thrilled for them." Her smile faded. "Jasp, I have to talk to you about something." She held out her phone.

Curious, he took it from her. He quickly read over the Bayside Blogger's article, clicked the phone off and looked Carissa in the eye.

"Is this true?" she asked, taking the phone and shoving it in her purse. "Did you really have a hand in me helping at your mother's party?"

He considered for a moment. She was never supposed to find out about that. No one was. Which didn't sound great when he put it that way. But he'd only been trying to help her.

Now was the time he needed to come clean. "Yes, it's true."

She deflated, slipping into one of the chairs around a small table in the corner of his office.

"How?" she asked. "I thought there had been a family emergency."

"There had. Only not a super bad one. Jasmine, the chef, found out her daughter broke her arm. I was snagging snacks in the kitchen when she took the call. She said her husband was there and she would work the party first and then leave at the first chance."

"But you convinced her to go early."

He nodded. "Yep."

"Jasper, what were you thinking? What if I had been late to the party? What if I hadn't stepped up to fill in that night? Your mother's party would have been ruined."

He followed her example and took a seat across from her. "I had complete faith in you. I still do."

Any remaining anger drained from her face. She reached out and cupped his cheek. "Thank you for that. But Jasp, you can't keep creating opportunities for me. That's not right."

"It was nothing. Just one night."

Her hand fell. "What about this café? Be honest. Did you do all of that for me, too?"

"No," he said adamantly, and meant it. "I really think this is a good addition to the town. Maybe I bucked tradition and good business practice by going straight to you for the café." He offered his best smile. "But you're just so damn good. You deserve this."

She bit her lip. "I haven't earned it."

"You will."

He watched as she wiped her palms on her legs. "That's a lot of pressure, Jasp. Plus, you have to let me do this myself. My way."

He leaned forward. "I am. The café is yours."

She let out a small laugh. "You own it."

"But you're running it. You make all the decisions. This is your baby."

Carissa frowned. "That's all I want. To be independent. To take care of myself." She cracked her knuckles. "In fact, I was thinking that maybe I could, I don't know, invest some of my own money into the café."

He glanced up at her, surprise evident on his face. "Do you have money to invest?"

"Not much," she admitted. "But I did get a small settlement from the divorce. Because my catering business took off faster than anticipated and I'm not paying rent at my aunt's cottage, I have a little to play with."

He nodded, apparently deep in thought. "Car, I don't want you to waste your money."

"It wouldn't be a waste. It would be an investment into our joint business."

And it would give her some semblance of control. The independence she craved. Jasper got it.

"I understand that. Listen, why don't we table all of this for now and talk about the café? The lawyer will be here soon for us to fill out the paperwork."

She nodded, but Jasper sensed something was still off. He didn't understand what bothered her so much. He was only trying to take care of her.

He put everything else out of his mind as they went over some legal documents. When the official business was over, he brought the conversation back around to the café.

"I have some ideas for the logo," Carissa said. "I was going to ask Elle to work up a couple options for me."

Jasper crossed to his desk and returned with a large poster board.

"What's that?" Carissa asked.

"I had our art department come up with a couple of possibilities." He showed her the board.

She peered at them and then met his gaze. "These aren't really what I was thinking."

"That's okay. They can make more for you. Although I think this one really pops." He pointed at his favorite logo. "It would look great up on a sign. Don't you think?"

"Well, I..."

"Oh, before I forget. I found a great web designer. He can fix up what you have now."

She sat up straight. "I made that website myself. I'm proud of it."

Yikes. He needed to tread lightly. Jasper was aware that sometimes he got a little overzealous. "You did a really great job. But now that you're expanding, you need to get something a little more professional."

"I don't even know this guy."

"He's a friend of a friend, but he's worked on a ton of my clients' websites. You'll like him."

A red blush was working its way up her neck. "I'm sure I will but that's not the point."

"Oh, one more thing," Jasper continued. "I've been thinking about your menus."

She sat up straighter. "The menus for my catering business?"

He nodded. "I have some small suggestions."

Carissa rose, paced to the window and returned to the table. "You have suggestions for the menus that I created? Me, the caterer? The area where I actually know exactly what I'm doing and that has nothing to do with your café?"

He observed her for a few moments. He could see that she was agitated. But he didn't understand why. He wanted this business to succeed for her.

"Like I said, I have small, tiny, minuscule suggestions." Another thought popped into his head. "Oh, and about the hours you set—"

She slapped her hands on the table between them. "Jasper, stop it."

His attention flew to her. The blush now covered her face. Red cheeks, alert eyes that had turned a much darker shade of gray sat across the table from him. "Stop what?"

"You're trying to control me."

"No, I'm not. I'm trying to help you." Wasn't he?

"Help me? By making every single decision for me? By completely ignoring all of the things I want to do?"

"That's not what I'm doing," he said, defensiveness coating his words.

"Yes, it is, and I don't want to work this way. I don't want to live this way." Her lip trembled. "In fact, I already have lived this way. That's how I wound up back in Bayside."

Anger smacked him right in the gut at that comment. "Are you comparing me to your ex-husband?" Now he rose and met her strong gaze.

She looked away. "Yes, I am, because you're acting just like him. 'Do this, Carissa. Act this way, Carissa. Choose this logo, these hours, this menu, Carissa.'"

Jasper felt like she'd slapped him. How could she compare him to her ex? He was nothing like…

He couldn't even finish the thought. Instead, he glanced down at his notes. All of the ideas he had for the café. Maybe, well, maybe there were some controlling elements at play. But he was doing this out of the goodness of his heart. He wanted her to succeed.

He took a step toward her but she retreated farther away. "Car, don't you get why I'm doing all this?"

She shook her head slowly, her eyes darkening. "No, I don't think I do."

The intercom on his desk rang out and Sherry's voice filled the room. "Mr. Dumont, your lawyer is here."

Carissa ran her hands over her face. Jasper pressed the button on the intercom. "One minute, Sherry." He pinned her with a stare. "Why don't we just sign the papers and discuss the rest of this later?"

She stood in the middle of the room, frozen. Her beautiful face was set in a stoic expression. Jasper would give anything to read her thoughts at the moment.

"Car?" he asked.

"I can't do this, Jasp. I'm sorry."

With that, she gathered up her belongings and quickly

made her way to the door. She couldn't do what? The café or their relationship? In either case, panic rose in his chest as he watched her walk away with his heart in her hand. For the second time in his life.

Chapter Eleven

Bayside Blogger @BSBlogger
What recently reunited couple is ALREADY calling it quits?
Check my blog for the full story.

Carissa would have liked to spend the entire day in bed.
Instead, she was surrounded by copious amounts of chocolate chips, bags of flour and sugar, and more butter wrap-
pers than one person ever needed to see in their lifetime.

Despite wanting to curl into a ball and mope for the
next week—or year—she'd promised Riley she would bake
cookies for the high school fund-raiser. She might have
walked out on Jasper and the Save the Day Café, but she
wouldn't let the kids down.

You'll just let Jasper down.

Every time she thought about Jasper, it felt like a very
large, strong fist was gripping her heart and clenching it
tightly. If she was honest with herself, she hadn't even felt
this way at the demise of her marriage.

"It doesn't make sense," she said as she took a break
from cookie-making and made a cup of tea.

She'd only been in a relationship with Jasper for a short time, and that relationship was supposed to be light and fun and not serious. She'd been with Preston for almost ten years. But when she compared the hurt from being cheated on to how she'd felt learning that Jasper had interfered in her life, the adultery took a back seat.

Because Jasper was so much more important to her than Preston had ever been. She guessed that the more you cared about someone, the harder it hurt. And it did hurt.

She knew she'd panicked. Pure and simple anxiety as she watched Jasper taking the reins of the café. Not to mention, learning that he'd interfered at his mother's party when she'd first arrived in town.

The frustrating part was that she knew it came from a good place with Jasper. Yet she still felt terrified. Carissa wanted her independence. She didn't want to rely on anyone. At some point yesterday, she'd been sitting in his office watching her life spin out of her control. Again.

It hadn't ended well the last time. As Jasper spit out names and possible vendors, she was transported back to her fancy Chicago condo with Preston.

"Of course I love it. But I just can't believe you bought an entire condo without consulting me."

"What are you talking about? I did this for you."

Hadn't Jasper said something similar yesterday? The problem was, she didn't want people to do things for her. She wanted—needed—to do them herself. Because if she didn't, she was following in her father's less-than-illustrious footsteps.

Now she'd run out on their business deal and had no idea where she stood with Jasper. She wished she could reflect on it more only… *Ding.* The oven timer reminded her why she didn't have time to dwell on the situation.

She took the sheet of chocolate chip cookies out of the

oven and shoved the next sheet in. After setting the timer, she turned back to the disaster she was currently calling a kitchen. There was no way she could get all of these cookies done in this one small kitchen, with one equally small oven, all by herself. What had she been thinking trying to open a café? Really, she was doing Jasper a favor by walking out on the contract signing.

"Stop thinking about Jasper. Focus."

Like that was going to happen. She so needed help. A knock sounded on the front door. As if on cue, Riley stood on the porch, wearing a darling outfit of skinny jeans, flats, a banana-yellow shirt, and a matching bright yellow scarf with lime-green polka dots around her neck.

"You look like something out of an old Audrey Hepburn movie," Carissa said by way of greeting.

"Why thank you." Riley beamed. "Not gonna lie. I've seen you look better." She eyed Carissa's outfit of pajama bottoms, ratty Northwestern T-shirt she'd had for a million years, and unbrushed hair piled on top of her head in a messy bun. If she had to guess, there was more than likely flour on her face and raw dough behind her ear.

Carissa let Riley inside. "Please tell me you're here to help. Please, please, please."

Riley put her hands up in front of her. "Whoa, girl. I've never seen you like this. Cool-as-a-cucumber Carissa never freaks out."

"Well, I've turned a new leaf. I'm in way over my head with these cookies."

Riley stood back and gave her a long once-over. "Cookies, I can help with. But…is there something else going on? You seem upset, and not just because of the baking."

Carissa was running her hands over her face, rubbing her tired eyes. In answer to Riley's question, she blurted,

"I think Jasper and I broke up." She hiccuped to hold in the tears that threatened.

Riley's face morphed from question to sympathy. She led Carissa to the couch and forced her to sit down. "I'm sorry. What happened? No, wait, we need Elle for both this conversation and the cookies. Give me a second." Riley whipped her phone out, then had a quick conversation with Elle. After, she brought Carissa's tea to her and made a cup for herself while they waited for Elle, who showed up fifteen minutes later.

"Good thing I just hired someone to help out at the gallery. Now, what's going on?" Elle said as she breezed in and sat on the other side of Carissa.

Flanked by her friends, Carissa sighed and then told them the entire story. She started all the way back in high school with her dad's antics and finished with her fight with Jasper in his office yesterday.

"It's like he didn't even see how controlling he was being. I know he was trying to help, but there was a point when I was sitting there that I thought about my future. And it resembled my dad's life," she finished in a quiet voice.

Riley raised a hand. "And there is the real issue."

"It really is, isn't it?" Carissa agreed. "It's not exactly the same scenario as my dad but there's this way in which I would be relying on someone else. It's Jasper's investment and it was all of his suggestions and ideas and none of mine. Plus, we're in a relationship. I would be dependent on him for everything."

Elle was tapping a finger to her lips as she considered. "On the one hand, it's kind of sweet. On the other, it's controlling and I get why you freaked."

Riley sat forward on the couch. "Where do you and Jasper stand now?"

The question set off a flurry of nerves in her stomach.

She shook her head. "I really don't know. I haven't talked to him." She clasped her hands together. "And I haven't heard from him, either. I think I really messed this up."

"You reacted honestly," Elle said. Her loyalty touched Carissa. "I'm surprised Jasper hasn't called or come over here."

"I'm not," Carissa admitted. She took a moment as her friends patiently waited for her explanation. "Jasper has always had an issue with being good enough. It started with his family and was exacerbated by our breakup after graduation. I basically rejected both the business deal he was so proud of and our relationship yesterday."

"That's not exactly what happened," Riley said.

"That's how he'll see it, though." Carissa knew him. He hadn't called because she'd hurt him.

Riley patted Carissa's hand. "I think you guys can work through this."

Could they? Carissa wasn't so sure. There was ten years of hurt and sadness and confusion between them. How could she be with someone who had the ability to get inside her so easily? Who could hurt her more than anyone else? Why would she allow that person in her life? Give them control over her emotions?

She was aware that both of her friends were eyeing her with concern. But she needed some time and space to work this out on her own. A master at changing the subject, she did just that.

"We have another problem," Carissa said. "A problem that might have a simpler solution." Elle narrowed her eyes and Riley leaned forward. "The cookies. One oven and mounds and mounds of raw dough. I need some help." She checked the clock on the TV. "With less than twenty-four hours to go."

"Oh, that," Riley said, swishing her hand through the

air as if this problem was nothing. "You got us. We can help bake."

Elle agreed. "I'll have to check in on the gallery throughout the day and go back to close up, but other than that, I'm here at your command. Put me to work."

Carissa let out a huge sigh of relief. "Thank you, thank you, thank you. And I'm sorry if I ruined whatever plans you had today."

"Don't be sorry," Riley said. "What do you say we put your independence issues and all things related to Jasper Dumont aside, and bake some damn cookies."

She couldn't help herself, Carissa grinned. "Now, that sounds like a plan."

"We are done," Riley said triumphantly.

Elle stretched her arms high over her head. "I can't believe we did it. I'll be seeing flour and sugar and sprinkles in my dreams for weeks, but we did it. How many did we make total?"

"One million," Riley answered around the peanut butter cookie she had just shoved into her mouth.

"Not quite that many, but close," Carissa put in.

She looked at each of her friends. Two women who hadn't been in her life a couple months ago. Now she couldn't imagine what she'd do without them. They'd stayed up the entire night mixing recipes, laying out cookies on trays, baking, and repeating the whole process over and over again. They'd consumed a whole extra-large pizza, countless cups of coffee and more cookie dough than was probably wise.

"Thank you both so much. Literally, I couldn't have done this without you."

"You're welcome. Now we have two hours to spare before the fund-raiser begins. I'm going to go home, make out with Cam for a little bit, and then take a shower."

"Same," Riley said as she crossed to the door. "You know, except for the making out with Cam part. And I think I'm going to plan another outfit around this scarf. It's fabulous and totally got wasted being here with you two all night."

Carissa laughed as she fingered the bright yellow material. "This scarf *is* fabulous and so are you."

Riley beamed. "See you guys at the high school."

Carissa waved goodbye from the door. Exhausted, she stood there a moment, taking in the fresh air. The weather had finally cooled off and she could smell the beginnings of fall. Leaves were just beginning to turn their autumnal colors. She might even need a jacket today.

Carissa didn't know how long she stood like that, one foot on the porch. But luckily the sound of her phone pulled her back in. Then she saw the name of the caller. Mom. Carissa sighed. She was way too tired for this. But manners had her saying hello anyway.

"Carissa, sweetheart, it's so good to hear your voice." Her mother's bright, cheery voice was so familiar and comforting that it had her heart longing for a hug.

How long had it been since she'd seen her parents? Too long. But it was so hard to be around her father. Every time she was, he'd go on and on about trips he'd taken and new things he'd bought.

"It's good to hear your voice, too, Mom. What's up?" She poured herself a glass of orange juice as she listened to her mother.

There was silence on the line. Never a good thing when dealing with her mother. Finally, her mom offered that mother of a mother line that had kids shaking everywhere. "Anything you want to tell me?"

Where to start, Carissa thought.

Instead, she decided to play it cool. "What do you want to know?"

"I'd like to know why my only child moved back to Bayside and didn't so much as mention it to her loving mother?"

Carissa bit her lip. It did sound bad when it was put like that. "Who spilled the beans?"

"Aunt Val mentioned it in passing. The question is, why didn't you?"

She shrugged but then remembered her mother couldn't see her. "I don't know, Mom. I made the decision pretty fast. I had to get out of Chicago."

"Because of the divorce?"

"Because of the divorce and the fact that I didn't have anywhere to live or any money or any friends or a job."

"Oh, baby. Why didn't you come here? We would have taken care of you."

Just like you took care of me when Dad spent all your money? Like how you left me to figure out higher education on my own? Like when you ripped everything away that I'd known my entire life at a very scary time?

She didn't say any of that, though. Sometimes old wounds were better left alone. "I wanted to figure it out for myself."

She could practically hear her mother's smile. Even through the technology of cell phones, she sensed her mother relax. "You always were independent."

Not always. Not during her marriage. "Well, I'm back in Bayside, living at Aunt Val's place while she travels the globe."

"I do miss Bayside. What's it like to be back there again?"

An image of Jasper flashed into her mind. "It's kind of the same. But kind of different, too."

They talked about the town and some of her mother's old friends. Carissa tried to catch her up on everything. She also told her mom about her desire to be a caterer. But at her mom's expressed pleasure, she started fidgeting. So she changed the subject. "What's going on with you, Mom?"

"Nothing much on my end. Just working hard."

After her parents left Bayside in shame, they'd moved to Portland, Maine. Her mother had held a series of positions; most recently she was working at a day care center. Her mother's bubbly attitude and aptitude to deal with children made the job a perfect fit, in Carissa's opinion.

"Where's Dad?"

"He's playing golf with a friend of his."

Of course he was. Her mother was carrying the load and her dad was out playing eighteen holes. He'd probably also placed some friendly wager on the outcome, too. "Whose money is he using for his golf game?"

"Oh, Carissa. Stop worrying about us. You do that far too much. Your father and I, we're fine."

Fine? Fine? Carissa shook her head. How could her mother say that they were fine? Nothing about her father's spending habits and her mother's blind eye was fine.

Carissa took a deep breath. "Don't you think that Dad should pull his weight? Wouldn't it be good for him to get a job of his own and help support you?"

"Your father's a good man."

"But, but," she stuttered. "He's made so many mistakes."

"So have I," her mother replied simply. "I didn't marry your father and stay with him all of these years because he was perfect."

That comment had her freezing in place. "Why did you stay with him all this time?"

"Because I love him."

Four small words. Carissa wanted to protest. She wanted

more of an answer than that. After everything they'd been through as a couple, how could her mother love him?

"I know how it must seem to you, Carissa. Like your father constantly messed up business deals and jobs."

Uh, yeah, pretty much.

"You don't know the whole story," her mother continued. "There were times your father did mess up of his own accord. But other times, there were circumstances that were out of our control. I know you don't want to hear it, but sometimes your dad was the victim."

"But, Mom—"

"Not always," she was quick to finish. "Life isn't always black and white."

It didn't make sense and she had a feeling it never would. Like always, she dug deep within herself to separate the pain and confusion her father evoked and the love she had for her mother.

Then her mom said something that took her by complete surprise. "I'm sorry about what happened to your college money, Carissa. I'm so very sorry you had to get all of those jobs and work as hard as you did."

"I'm not." She realized for the first time she actually meant that.

There had been days where she'd worked early in the morning, gone to classes and study groups, and then finished her day at a different job. It had been hard, but it had also taught her so much.

Another realization hit. Before college, she'd been a pampered and sheltered teenager. Because of what she'd learned during that time at Northwestern, she was able to build her company today.

Her mother continued. "If it had been up to me, you would have floated into college on a cloud and lived in a protective bubble for four years." She let out a little laugh.

"I suppose all parents want that for their children. I didn't want you to want for anything."

"It was better the way it was. Trust me, Mom."

They spoke a little while longer before hanging up.

Then Carissa stood in the kitchen with half a glass of orange juice and the makings of a killer headache. She needed to take a shower and get ready for the fund-raiser. But she couldn't seem to move her feet. Somehow, she felt relieved and renewed after the conversation with her mother. Everything came back to one statement her mother had made.

Because I love him. The phrase echoed throughout her mind over and over. No qualms. No conditions. Her mother loved her father and that was it.

Carissa dropped the glass she was holding, the shards of glass raining onto the countertop she'd just cleaned. But she was too amazed at the epiphany she'd just had to worry about some broken glass.

For all of these years, Carissa had been searching for perfection. That's why she'd dated and subsequently married Preston. She'd wanted perfection and she'd gotten it. Only, life hadn't been quite so perfect. Preston had the pedigree and the manners. He was smart and handsome. They lived in the picture-perfect condo with the gorgeous view of the Chicago skyline. Their parties were attended by the best people. They drove the right cars. They belonged to the right clubs. They played the part just right.

Only it had been very, very wrong.

Her perfect-on-paper husband had been a massive disappointment off the page.

Then, there was Jasper. She always seemed to return to him. Not just her body, but her thoughts, her feelings. Even in college, he never strayed far from her musings. During her marriage, she would find Jasper creeping in to remind her of a much happier time.

She'd walked out on him and the café deal because he'd scared her. She loved him so he, and he alone, had the ability to hurt her more than anyone else. More than her dad even. And still, she wanted to be with him. He drove her crazy and she longed for him. Why?

"Because I love him," she said into the silence of the kitchen, echoing her mother's earlier statement. "I love Jasper."

She ran a hand through her hair. *Ohmigod, I love Jasper.* She started giggling uncontrollably as she wondered when it had happened. Maybe she'd never stopped loving him from back in high school. It didn't really matter because despite everything, she was in love with him now. More importantly, she realized that loving someone meant loving all of them, imperfections and all. After all, she had a lot of imperfections and Jasper seemed to look past them.

She may not understand her parents' relationship. She definitely didn't get how her mother could put up with her father's lack of ambition and general laziness. But it wasn't up to her. After that phone call, she understood that her mother loved her father anyway. In spite of everything life had thrown at them.

And she loved Jasper Dumont in the same careless, crazy, makes-no-sense kind of way. At one time, she'd thought that her ex-husband was the polar opposite of her father. But she'd been wrong. Jasper was the one who represented everything her father didn't.

Now she had to figure out how to tell him and hope that she hadn't pushed him away too much the other day.

Jasper walked through one of the side doors to his alma mater. It smelled of school—pencils, erasers, gym shoes. He glanced around the hallway. The lockers had been upgraded since his time here. But the large overhead light still flickered like it had when he'd been a student. Were they never going to fix it?

Jasper continued down the hallway. He knew it was still the same old Bayside High and yet it seemed smaller somehow. Maybe because this was no longer the center of his universe. That had been a different era where things like study hall, baseball practice and Carissa Blackwell were the most important things on his mind.

Well, maybe one of those things was still in the forefront of his mind.

He continued toward the gymnasium. The last thing he wanted to do today was show up for this date auction. He hadn't slept in two nights and felt like crap. But he'd promised Riley before Carissa had even returned to town, and he wouldn't go back on that. Even though he really didn't want to go out with anyone but Carissa. Was that ever going to happen again? Jasper still didn't get what had gone down in his office. One minute they'd been discussing the café. The next, she'd been accusing him of controlling her life and walking away from him.

And once again, he felt like he hadn't been good enough. Like all of his work and all of his planning wasn't enough.

Worse was the fact that her words had the ability to make him feel the way he used to when he'd originally walked through these hallways. Fun Jasper Dumont who everyone likes but no one takes seriously.

Cam came around the corner from the opposite direction as Jasper reached the gym. Cam's face fell instantly. "What's wrong?" he asked.

Jasper shook his head. "Nothing. Just gearing up to be a piece of meat."

Cam placed a firm hand on Jasper's shoulder and steered him away from the gym's door. "Cut the crap, Jasp. What happened?"

He shrugged first, but the next thing he knew he was spilling the entire story. "In conclusion, well, I don't really know what the conclusion is or where we stand." He let out a harsh laugh. "I wasn't ambitious enough back in high school and I guess now I'm too ambitious." He threw his hands up in the air. "Can't win. But the bookstore and café is a great idea. Now I have to figure out how to proceed." *Without Carissa.* Jasper looked down at his feet. If he hadn't, he may have anticipated the slap upside the head from his brother. "Hey, what was that?"

"Did that knock any sense into you? Because there's more where that came from. Stop feeling sorry for yourself."

"I'm not…" He trailed off. He couldn't finish the sentence because he was, in fact, feeling sorry for himself.

"Nothing to say?" Cam goaded.

"Fine, I'm being indulgent. But who cares. The woman I love didn't accept what I offered her and walked out on me."

Love? Yes, love. He still loved Carissa.

Cam's face softened. "Oh, Jasp."

Anger suddenly took over. "What? It's not like you didn't know." For extra emphasis, he gave a good hard push squarely in his brother's chest. "Tell me you didn't know."

Cam was shaking his head as he said, "Christ, Jasp, everyone knew. You love her and she loves you."

"She doesn't love—"

"Don't even finish that sentence, bro. The only two people in Bayside who are unaware of their feelings are you and Carissa."

Jasper wanted to lash out. Instead, he sank back against the lockers, exhausted. "Answer me this. If she loves me, then why did she react that way when I offered her such a great opportunity?"

Cam shook his head. "I love you, but you are incredibly stupid."

"Hey," Jasper protested. "I'm hurting here."

"You're hurting because you're an idiot. And it sounds like Carissa is screwing you again." Cam held up a restraining hand as Jasper straightened. "I'm sorry but I think she left you hanging high and dry just like she did back in high school."

"It's not like that, Cam. There are other things at play here. Issues with her parents. Her dad, in particular. And you don't even know the reason why she broke up with me after graduation."

"Do you?"

"Yes, we talked about it. It's all tied to those issues."

Cam rolled back on his heels and leveled Jasper with a firm stare.

"What?"

"Did you hear what you just said?"

Jasper replayed their conversation. He didn't detect anything special.

Cam punched him in the arm. "She has issues. Issues that made her run from you once already."

"I just told you that."

"You really are dense. If she ran from you once due to her own personal demons, might that be the same reason she's doing it again?"

"Well…huh." He hadn't thought of it that way.

"She's not rejecting you, Jasp. She's protecting herself."

"But that's what I was trying to do by setting up this café for her. By helping her get everything started."

"Helping? Or controlling?" Cam laughed. "I know you, Jasp. You run in at full speed and try to help so much that you end up taking over. Maybe that's not what she needs."

It most certainly wasn't. He was an idiot.

"Come to your senses yet?"

"Seems like it."

"Then, go get your girl." With that, he shoved his hands in his pockets and walked down the hall to the gym, whistling while he left Jasper with a lot to think about.

When had Cam become so damn wise? Had to be Elle's doing. Cam had never been in touch with his emotions—or anyone else's, for that matter—before Elle came along.

He exhaled and ran a hand over his face. But the truth was that he did love Carissa. And he hoped Cam was right and she loved him, too. He hadn't meant to force his idea on her. It really had come from a good place.

He started walking toward the gym but suddenly froze. Maybe it had been for himself a bit, too. Maybe he had come on strong. Maybe he should have listened to her more and not forced his opinions.

"Dumont, there you are."

He turned to see Riley's bubbly face bouncing toward him. "Did you just call me Dumont?"

She slapped him on the arm. "It's the gym, I'm telling you. Makes me feel all masculine."

He chuckled. "Nice scarf," he commented. Riley was always dressed to the nines. Today she wore all black with a pop of color from a bright yellow scarf with lime-green polka dots tied around her neck.

"Thanks. I'm going for dramatic effect for my emcee outfit."

"That means you didn't decide to cancel this whole date auction then?"

Riley chucked him under his chin. "And disappoint all the women of Bayside? I expect you to bring in the most money."

"That's a lot of pressure." He followed her into the gym and was immediately assaulted by the usual suspects. His mother and her friends were all dancing around him, offering advice for the auction and pledging their desire to bid on him, all while his brother and Elle stood hand in hand against the wall with identical grins as they watched him. He offered a finger of choice in his brother's direction just before Riley led him onto the stage.

"Hey, Ri, have you, um, seen Carissa lately?" he whispered so none of the other bachelors would hear.

Her eyes instantly softened as she looked his way. "As a matter of fact, I have."

He waited but Riley didn't give in. "And?" he asked.

"And I think the two of you should talk. Like, really talk."

"Apparently, that's a popular idea," he said drily. He searched the gym, hoping for a glance of Carissa. Even if he couldn't see the rows of tables in the back of the gym filled to the brim with cookies, his nose would have alerted him. This was definitely the best this gym had ever smelled. It also meant that Carissa had to be around somewhere. "Is she here?"

Riley opened her mouth but before she could say anything, her name was called. She needed to go to the podium to begin the auction. "We'll talk afterward," she promised.

He nodded because what else could he do?

The auction began but Jasper spent most of it in a blur. He knew every single bachelor up on stage. Heck, he also knew almost every single person crammed into the gym to witness this spectacle. But he kept his eyes trained on the tables of cookies in the back of the gym. Surely Carissa would show up at some point.

Riley seemed to be doing a great job as emcee, offering stats and hobbies of each of the bachelors. She had people placed around the gym to help her as arm after arm shot into the air, pledging money in exchange for a date with Bayside's finest.

One of the men to bring in the most bids was Sawyer Wallace, editor of the Bayside Bugle. Interestingly, he was promised to Simone, who seemed ecstatic she'd won. As they marched off together, Jasper noticed a rare frown on Riley's usually happy face.

But she pulled herself together quickly and announced the last bachelor of the day. Jasper didn't even realize it was his name being called until he felt someone push him from behind and he stumbled onstage.

"Ah, here's the man everyone's been waiting for. Making quite the entrance, it's Jasper Dumont."

A round of applause, along with the obligatory catcalls, sounded. Jasper took his first mark, having been trained by Riley the other day. They had three different marks to hit while Riley read out their stats. He felt like an idiot standing there as people stared at him.

"Jasper Dumont is one of Bayside's most eligible bachelors. Besides running Dumont Incorporated, Jasper enjoys coffee from The Brewside, graphic novels, baseball and long, romantic walks on the beach."

Jasper turned and shot Riley an annoyed look. He most certainly had not said that about the beach walks. She snickered and continued reading her stats, only half of which were true.

When she finished, he took center stage to thunderous applause. He noticed his mother was standing front and center.

The bidding began at twenty dollars. It quickly rose to forty.

"Forty-five," one of his mother's friends offered.

"Fifty." Jasper almost choked at his old high school English teacher's bid.

"Fifty-five." Lilah Dumont jumped up and down excitedly.

"You can't bid on me, Mom," Jasper said through clenched teeth. Everyone laughed.

Once the figure got up to one hundred dollars, a bidding war ensued. Both women were beautiful and a couple months ago, Jasper would have been glowing from the attention and the opportunity to go out with either one of them.

But at the moment, he couldn't seem to find any excitement in the idea of sharing a meal with anyone but Carissa. His gaze drifted over to the cookie tables and once again he was disappointed to see they remained Carissa-less.

"Ladies, ladies, let's keep it G-rated," Riley was saying. "There are kids here today. We're up to two hundred dollars and the fight seems to be narrowed down to Jenny Heatherlea and Trina Wingate. Do I hear two-ten?"

"Two-ten."

Everyone, including Jasper, turned to the side entrance of the gym as the new voice rang out over the crowd. He heard a few gasps at the sight of Carissa.

"Hey, that's not fair," Jenny, one of the women bidding on him, called out. "She just got here."

"And they used to date," Trina, the other woman, complained. "She has an advantage."

Riley tried to calm the crowd down from the podium. "There are no exclusions in this auction. Anyone is free to bid. Let's continue."

"I heard they're still dating." This came from Tony from The Brewside, who had donated coffee and tea for the event. "According to the Bayside Blogger."

"Thanks, man," Jasper called out.

Tony offered a grin in exchange, clearly enjoying himself.

"Nope, they broke up again. Didn't you see Facebook today?" someone else called out.

"In any case, we are going to accept Carissa's bid," Riley continued. "Even though she's starting her own business and really shouldn't be spending any extra money at the moment."

Jasper would have chuckled at Riley's commentary if he wasn't so entranced by Carissa's entrance. She looked beautiful, as always. Today she had on tight jeans, a bright red sweater and tall, sexy boots. But she also looked tired. Even from across the gym, he could see the strain on her face, the shadows under her eyes. She wove her fingers together nervously as she bit her lip.

Part of Jasper wanted to rush to her. He wanted to pull her into his arms and never let go. Another part of him felt cautious, unsure of what she was thinking. To be honest, he was still a little hurt. And yet there was a glimmer of hope. She'd shown up and bid on him.

"Last bid was two hundred and ten dollars. Do I hear two-fifteen?" Riley asked the crowd.

"Three hundred dollars," one of the women shouted. The rest of the crowd offered a collective "ooohhhh."

Riley looked toward Carissa, who was frowning. Jasper knew she didn't have the money to do this.

"Four hundred," the other bidder screamed.

Holy crap, Jasper thought.

"My, what generosity we're seeing today," Riley said. "We have an offer of four hundred dollars for Jasper Dumont."

"Five hundred," Jenny said. "I always win," she added with a determined look toward Trina, who threw her hands in the air and backed up. She was out.

So it was between Jenny, who always won, and Carissa.

When Jasper turned in Carissa's direction though, she was nowhere in sight. His heart sank.

"Okay," Riley said uncertainly, also noticing that her friend was absent. "We have five hundred dollars for Jasper Dumont. Do I hear five-ten?"

"No."

Everyone flung around to face the back of the gym where Carissa now stood. She was next to one of the cookie tables.

She'd said no. Jasper wanted to melt into the stage.

Then Carissa grabbed two of the cookies and held them high in the air. "I don't have five hundred and ten dollars. But I do have cookies. I bid all of these peanut butter cookies."

"She can't do that," Jenny said.

"I don't know. These cookies are pretty good." This was said by George from the Rusty Keg, who had cookie crumbs embedded in his beard.

"I offer my chocolate chip cookies, the oatmeal raisin, the shortbread." Carissa was walking forward as she spoke. "I give you all of my coconut bars, the white chocolate macadamia nut." She handed the two cookies she still held to Cam as she walked by, her eyes now clasped onto Jasper's.

"I give you the brownies I made, both the regular and the double-chocolate caramel ones. And…and…well, that's everything I made for today. But I will make you anything you want, Jasp."

She spread her arms wide, offering herself to him. Jasper realized how huge the gesture was for her, so he jumped off the stage and met her halfway.

"All of this for one date with me?" he asked her.

"Well," she said in a quiet voice, lowering it so only he could hear. "I was hoping for more than one date."

"The café," he began. "I'm sorry I was so controlling and that I…"

She held up a hand to stop him. "I want to do the café, Jasp. You challenge me and I know you only wanted what's best for me."

"Hey, can you guys speak up? We can't hear you," George called out. Everyone started chuckling, but Jasper softened his voice even more.

"I was trying to help you, because I love helping the people I care about."

"One of your best qualities." Red tinged her cheeks as she glanced around at all of the people watching them. "I overreacted."

"That's not true—" he began, but she cut him off.

"I was blaming you for other things in my life and… well, it doesn't matter. Because you're not my father. You're not my ex."

"What am I then?"

Her gaze drilled into his. "You're the person I want to be with."

He was having a hell of a time staying calm. "I'm not perfect, Car."

A tear spilled over onto her cheek. "Thank God." With that she launched herself into his arms and held on tight. "I want you, Jasper. Just the way you are."

"Good," he whispered into her ear. "Because I love you, Car. I did back then and I do now."

"I love you, too." She pressed her lips to his to the sound of monstrous applause.

"Well, folks, I think we have our winner for Jasper Dumont. Sorry, Jenny," Riley said from the stage, not sounding sorry at all. There were tears shining in her eyes.

The crowd kept clapping and whistling but Jasper couldn't care less. He felt like the luckiest man alive. Carissa beamed up at him even as her eyes shone with un-shed tears.

He might be back in his old high school, but everything was different now. Today, he felt like a new man. A happy man, who couldn't believe how fortunate he was to have the woman of his dreams standing in his arms.

Epilogue

Life is sweet, dear Bayside.
How can you not think that after watching Carissa and Jasper in the gym earlier today? Seems like they got over their issues and let each other in. No doubt another happy ending. And too bad for Jenny and Trina, who I heard were both drowning their sorrows in the dozens of cookies they purchased after the auction…

From her seat in The Brewside, the Bayside Blogger sat back, perusing her screen and what she'd just typed. She was happy about Carissa and Jasper. And she liked to think that she had something to do with their reunion. Sometimes people just needed a little push. After all, where would Bayside be without her meddling? Some people may claim to get annoyed but honestly, she only nudged where she saw a need. And Carissa and Jasper had definitely needed a big fat shove.

Now they were together. They'd left the gym hand in hand, right behind big brother Cam and Elle. Two other people who'd needed some help to get to their happy ending.

The Bayside Blogger reread her column again, made some tweaks, and then hit Post. Now that the Dumont brothers were taken care of, perhaps it was time to focus on herself. Maybe it was her turn to find love.

Luckily she didn't do a video blog or everyone would see the frown on her face. Like most people, she'd been through her own ordeal. Did she deserve love? She wasn't sure.

Shaking her head, she tried to dispel the sudden dark mood. After all, today was a good day. She'd helped two more people get together. For now, that would have to be enough.

Her story was one for another day.

Packing up her laptop, she rose, flinging her computer bag over her shoulder and reaching for her purse. She gave a little wave to Tony, who offered a smile and wave back.

As she pushed through the door and smiled at the sound of the melodious chimes, she had no idea that she'd left her bright yellow scarf with lime-green polka dots on the table...

* * * * *

*Will the Bayside Blogger find her own
happily-ever-after?
And will she be unmasked—finally?*

Don't miss

SMITTEN WITH THE BOSS

the next installment of
SAVED BY THE BLOG
*Kerri Carpenter's new miniseries for
Harlequin Special Edition*

*On sale January 2018, wherever
Harlequin books and ebooks are sold.*

*Julia Winston is looking to conquer life,
not become heartbreaker Jamie Caine's
latest conquest. But when two young brothers
wind up in Julia's care for the holidays,
she'll take any help she can get—even Jamie's.*

Read on for a preview of
New York Times *bestselling author
RaeAnne Thayne's SUGAR PINE TRAIL,
the latest installment in her beloved*
HAVEN POINT *series.*

CHAPTER ONE

THIS WAS GOING to be a disaster.

Julia Winston stood in her front room looking out the lace curtains framing her bay window at the gleaming black SUV parked in her driveway like a sleek, predatory beast.

Her stomach jumped with nerves, and she rubbed suddenly clammy hands down her skirt. Under what crazy moon had she ever thought this might be a good idea? She must have been temporarily out of her head.

Those nerves jumped into overtime when a man stepped out of the vehicle and stood for a moment, looking up at her house.

Jamie Caine.

Tall, lean, hungry.

Gorgeous.

Now the nerves felt more like nausea. What had she done? The moment Eliza Caine called and asked her if her brother-in-law could rent the upstairs apartment of Winston House, she should have told her friend in no uncertain terms that the idea was preposterous. Utterly impossible.

As usual, Julia had been weak and indecisive, and when

Eliza told her it was only for six weeks—until January, when the condominium Jamie Caine was buying in a new development along the lake would be finished—she had wavered.

He needed a place to live, and she *did* need the money. Anyway, it was only for six weeks. Surely she could tolerate having the man living upstairs in her apartment for six weeks—especially since he would be out of town for much of those six weeks as part of his duties as lead pilot for the Caine Tech company jet fleet.

The reality of it all was just beginning to sink in, though. Jamie Caine, upstairs from her, in all his sexy, masculine glory.

She fanned herself with her hand, wondering if she was having a premature-onset hot flash or if her new furnace could be on the fritz. The temperature in here seemed suddenly off the charts.

How would she tolerate having him here, spending her evenings knowing he was only a few steps away and that she would have to do her best to hide the absolutely ridiculous, truly humiliating crush she had on the man?

This was such a mistake.

Heart pounding, she watched through the frothy curtains as he pulled a long black duffel bag from the back of his SUV and slung it over his shoulder, lifted a laptop case over the other shoulder, then closed the cargo door and headed for the front steps.

A moment later, her old-fashioned musical doorbell echoed through the house. If she hadn't been so nervous, she might have laughed at the instant reaction of the three cats, previously lounging in various states of boredom around the room. The moment the doorbell rang, Empress and Tabitha both jumped off the sofa as if an electric current had just zipped through it, while Audrey Hepburn arched her back and bushed out her tail.

"That's right, girls. We've got company. It's a man, believe it or not, and he's moving in upstairs. Get ready."

The cats sniffed at her with their usual disdainful look. Empress ran in front of her, almost tripping her on the way to answer the door—on purpose, she was quite sure.

With her mother's cats darting out ahead of her, Julia walked out into what used to be the foyer of the house before she had created the upstairs apartment and now served as an entryway to both residences. She opened the front door, doing her best to ignore the rapid tripping of her heartbeat.

"Hi. You're Julia, right?"

As his sister-in-law was one of her dearest friends, she and Jamie had met numerous times at various events at Snow Angel Cove and elsewhere, but she didn't bother reminding him of that. Julia knew she was eminently forgettable. Most of the time, that was just the way she liked it.

"Yes. Hello, Mr. Caine."

He aimed his high-wattage killer smile at her. "Please. Jamie. Nobody calls me Mr. Caine."

Julia was grimly aware of her pulse pounding in her ears and a strange hitch in her lungs. Up close, Jamie Caine was, in a word, breathtaking. He was Mr. Darcy, Atticus Finch, Rhett Butler and Tom Cruise in *Top Gun* all rolled into one glorious package.

Dark hair, blue eyes and that utterly charming Caine smile he shared with Aidan, Eliza's husband, and the other Caine brothers she had met at various events.

"You were expecting me, right?" he said after an awkward pause. She jolted, suddenly aware she was staring and had left him standing entirely too long on her front step. She was an idiot. "Yes. Of course. Come in. I'm sorry."

Pull yourself together. He's just a guy who happens to be gorgeous.

So far she was seriously failing at Landlady 101. She sucked in a breath and summoned her most brisk keep-your-voice-down-please librarian persona.

"As you can see, we will share the entry. Because the home is on the registry of historical buildings, I couldn't put in an outside entrance to your apartment, as I might have preferred. The house was built in 1880, one of the earliest brick homes on Lake Haven. It was constructed by an ancestor of mine, Sir Robert Winston, who came from a wealthy British family and made his own fortune supplying timber to the railroads. He also invested in one of the first hot-springs resorts in the area. The home is Victorian, specifically in the spindled Queen Anne style. It consists of seven bedrooms and four bathrooms. When those bathrooms were added in the 1920s, they provided some of the first indoor plumbing in the region."

"Interesting," he said, though his expression indicated he found it anything but.

She was rambling, she realized, as she tended to do when she was nervous.

She cleared her throat and pointed to the doorway, where the three cats were lined up like sentinels, watching him with unblinking stares. "Anyway, through those doors is my apartment and yours is upstairs. I have keys to both doors for you along with a packet of information here."

She glanced toward the ornate marble-top table in the entryway—that her mother claimed once graced the mansion of Leland Stanford on Nob Hill in San Francisco—where she thought she had left the information. Unfortunately, it was bare. "Oh. Where did I put that? I must have left it inside in my living room. Just a moment."

The cats weren't inclined to get out of her way, so she

stepped over them, wondering if she came across as eccentric to him as she felt, a spinster librarian living with cats in a crumbling house crammed with antiques, a space much too big for one person.

After a mad scan of the room, she finally found the two keys along with the carefully prepared file folder of instructions atop the mantel, nestled amid her collection of porcelain angels. She had no recollection of moving them there, probably due to her own nervousness at having Jamie Caine moving upstairs.

She swooped them up and hurried back to the entry, where she found two of the cats curled around his leg, while Audrey was in his arms, currently being petted by his long, square-tipped fingers.

She stared. The cats had no time or interest in her. She only kept them around because her mother had adored them, and Julia couldn't bring herself to give away Mariah's adored pets. Apparently no female—human or feline—was immune to Jamie Caine. She should have expected it.

"Nice cats."

Julia frowned. "Not usually. They're standoffish and bad tempered to most people."

"I guess I must have the magic touch."

So the Haven Point rumor mill said about him, anyway. "I guess you do," she said. "I found your keys and information about the apartment. If you would like, I can show you around upstairs."

"Lead on."

He offered a friendly smile, and she told herself that shiver rippling down her spine was only because the entryway was cooler than her rooms.

"This is a lovely house," he said as he followed her up the staircase. "Have you lived here long?"

"Thirty-two years in February. All my life, in other words."

Except the first few days, anyway, when she had still been in the Oregon hospital where her parents adopted her, and the three years she had spent at Boise State.

"It's always been in my family," she continued. "My father was born here and his father before him."

She was a Winston only by adoption but claimed her parents' family trees as her own and respected and admired their ancestors and the elegant home they had built here.

At the second-floor landing, she unlocked the apartment that had been hers until she moved down to take care of her mother after Mariah's first stroke, two years ago. A few years after taking the job at the Haven Point library, she had redecorated the upstairs floor of the house. It had been her way of carving out her own space.

Yes, she had been an adult living with her parents. Even as she might have longed for some degree of independence, she couldn't justify moving out when her mother had so desperately needed her help with Julia's ailing father.

Anyway, she had always figured it wasn't the same as most young adults who lived in their parents' apartments. She'd had an entire self-contained floor to herself. If she wished, she could shop on her own, cook on her own, entertain her friends, all without bothering her parents.

Really, it had been the best of all situations—close enough to help, yet removed enough to live her own life. Then her father died and her mother became frail herself, and Julia had felt obligated to move downstairs to be closer, in case her mother needed her.

Now, as she looked at her once-cherished apartment, she tried to imagine how Jamie Caine would see these rooms, with the graceful reproduction furniture and the pastel wall colors and the soft carpet and curtains.

Oddly, the feminine decorations only served to emphasize how very *male* Jamie Caine was, in contrast.

She did her best to ignore that unwanted observation.

"This is basically the same floor plan as my rooms below, with three bedrooms, as well as the living room and kitchen," she explained. "You've got an en suite bathroom off the largest bedroom and another one for the other two bedrooms."

"Wow. That's a lot of room for one guy."

"It's a big house," she said with a shrug. She had even more room downstairs, factoring in the extra bedroom in one addition and the large south-facing sunroom.

Winston House was entirely too rambling for one single woman and three bad-tempered cats. It had been too big for an older couple and their adopted daughter. It had been too large when it was just her and her mother, after her father died.

The place had basically echoed with emptiness for the better part of a year after her mother's deteriorating condition had necessitated her move to the nursing home in Shelter Springs. Her mother had hoped to return to the house she had loved, but that never happened, and Mariah Winston died four months ago.

Julia missed her every single day.

"Do you think it will work for you?" she asked.

"It's more than I need, but should be fine. Eliza told you this is only temporary, right?"

Julia nodded. She was counting on it. Then she could find a nice, quiet, older lady to rent who wouldn't leave her so nervous.

"She said your apartment lease ran out before your new condo was finished."

"Yes. The development was supposed to be done two months ago, but the builder has suffered delay after delay.

I've already extended my lease twice. I didn't want to push my luck with my previous landlady by asking for a third extension."

All Jamie had to do was smile at the woman and she likely would have extended his lease again without quibbling. And probably would have given him anything else he wanted, too.

Julia didn't ask why he chose not to move into Snow Angel Cove with his brother Aidan and Aidan's wife, Eliza, and their children. It was none of her business, anyway. The only thing she cared about was the healthy amount he was paying her in rent, which would just about cover the new furnace she had installed a month earlier.

"It was a lucky break for me when Eliza told me you were considering taking on a renter for your upstairs space."

He aimed that killer smile at her again, and her core muscles trembled from more than just her workout that morning.

If she wasn't very, very careful, she would end up making a fool of herself over the man.

It took effort, but she fought the urge to return his smile. This was business, she told herself. That was all. She had something he needed, a place to stay, and he was willing to pay for it. She, in turn, needed funds if she wanted to maintain this house that had been in her family for generations.

"It works out for both of us. You've already signed the rental agreement outlining the terms of your tenancy and the rules."

She held out the information packet. "Here you'll find all the information you might need, information like internet access, how to work the electronics and the satellite television channels, garbage pickup day and mail delivery. Do you have any other questions?"

Business, she reminded herself, making her voice as no-nonsense and brisk as possible.

"I can't think of any now, but I'm sure something will come up."

He smiled again, but she thought perhaps this time his expression was a little more reserved. Maybe he could sense she was un-charmable.

Or so she wanted to tell herself, anyway.

"I would ask that you please wipe your feet when you carry your things in and out, given the snow out there. The stairs are original wood, more than a hundred years old."

Cripes. She sounded like a prissy spinster librarian.

"I will do that, but I don't have much to carry in. Since El told me the place is furnished, I put almost everything in storage." He gestured to the duffel and laptop bag, which he had set inside the doorway. "Besides this, I've only got a few more boxes in the car."

"In that case, here are your keys. The large one goes to the outside door. The smaller one is for your apartment. I keep the outside door locked at all times. You can't be too careful."

"True enough."

She glanced at her watch. "I'm afraid I've already gone twenty minutes past my lunch hour and must return to the library. My cell number is written on the front of the packet, in case of emergency."

"Looks like you've covered everything."

"I think so." Yes, she was a bit obsessively organized, and she didn't like surprises. Was anything wrong with that?

"I hope you will be comfortable here," she said, then tried to soften her stiff tone with a smile that felt every bit as awkward. "Good afternoon."

"Uh, same to you."

Her heart was still pounding as she nodded to him and hurried for the stairs, desperate for escape from all that… masculinity.

She rushed back downstairs and into her apartment for her purse, wishing she had time to splash cold water on her face.

However would she get through the next six weeks with him in her house?

HE WAS *NOT* looking forward to the next six weeks.

Jamie stood in the corner of the main living space to the apartment he had agreed to rent, sight unseen.

Big mistake.

It was roomy and filled with light, that much was true. But the decor was too…fussy…for a man like him, all carved wood and tufted upholstery and pastel wall colorings.

It wasn't exactly his scene, more like the kind of place a repressed, uppity librarian might live.

As soon as he thought the words, Jamie frowned at himself. That wasn't fair. She might not have been overflowing with warmth and welcome, but Julia Winston had been very polite to him—especially since he knew she hadn't necessarily wanted to rent to him.

This was what happened when he gave his sister-in-law free rein to find him an apartment in the tight local rental market. She had been helping him out, since he had been crazy busy the last few weeks flying Caine Tech execs from coast to coast—and all places in between—as they worked on a couple of big mergers.

Eliza had wanted him to stay at her and Aidan's rambling house by the lake. The place was huge, and they had plenty of room, but while he loved his older brother Aidan and his wife and kids, Jamie preferred his own space. He didn't much care what that space looked like, especially when it was temporary.

With time running out on his lease extension, he had been relieved when Eliza called him via Skype the week before to tell him she had found him something more than suitable, for a decent rent.

"You'll love it!" Eliza had beamed. "It's the entire second floor of a gorgeous old Victorian in that great neighborhood on Snow Blossom Lane, with a simply stunning view of the lake."

"Sounds good," he had answered.

"You'll be upstairs from my friend Julia Winston, and, believe me, you couldn't ask for a better landlady. She's sweet and kind and perfectly wonderful. You know Julia, right?"

When he had looked blankly at her and didn't immediately respond, his niece Maddie had popped her face into the screen from where she had been apparently listening in off camera. "You know! She's the library lady. She tells all the stories!"

"Ah. *That* Julia," he'd said, not bothering to mention to his seven-year-old niece that in more than a year of living in town, he had somehow missed out on story time at the Haven Point library.

He also didn't mention to Maddie's mother that he only vaguely remembered Julia Winston. Now that he had seen her again, he understood why. She was the kind of woman who tended to slip into the background—and he had the odd impression that wasn't accidental.

She wore her brown hair past her shoulders, without much curl or style to it and held back with a simple black band, and she appeared to use little makeup to play up her rather average features.

She did have lovely eyes, he had to admit. Extraordinary,

even. They were a stunning blue, almost violet, fringed by naturally long eyelashes.

Her looks didn't matter, nor did the decor of her house. He would only be here a few weeks, then he would be moving into his new condo.

She clearly didn't like him. He frowned, wondering how he might have offended Julia Winston. He barely remembered even meeting the woman, but he must have done something for her to be so cool to him.

A few times during that odd interaction, she had alternated between seeming nervous to be in the same room with him to looking at him with her mouth pursed tightly, as if she had just caught him spreading peanut butter across the pages of *War and Peace*.

She was entitled to her opinion. Contrary to popular belief, he didn't need everyone to like him.

His brothers would probably say it was good for him to live upstairs from a woman so clearly immune to his charm.

One thing was clear: he now had one more reason to be eager for his condo to be finished.

Don't miss
SUGAR PINE TRAIL
by RaeAnne Thayne
Available October 2017 from HQN Books!

COMING NEXT MONTH FROM

H HARLEQUIN®

SPECIAL EDITION

Available October 17, 2017

#2581 THE RANCHER'S CHRISTMAS SONG
The Cowboys of Cold Creek • by RaeAnne Thayne
Music teacher Ella Baker doesn't have time to corral rancher Beckett McKinley's two wild boys. But when they ask her to teach them a song for their father, she manages to wrangle some riding lessons out of the deal. Still, Ella and Beckett come from two different worlds, and it might take a Christmas miracle to finally bring them together.

#2582 THE MAVERICK'S SNOWBOUND CHRISTMAS
Montana Mavericks: The Great Family Roundup
by Karen Rose Smith
Rancher Eli Dalton believes that visiting vet Hadley Strickland is just the bride he's been searching for! But can he heal her broken heart in time for the perfect holiday proposal?

#2583 A COWBOY FAMILY CHRISTMAS
Rocking Chair Rodeo • by Judy Duarte
When Drew Madison, a handsome rodeo promoter, meets the temporary cook at the Rocking Chair Ranch, the avowed bachelor falls for the lovely Lainie Montoya. But things get complicated when he learns she's the mystery woman who broke up his sister's marriage!

#2584 SANTA'S SEVEN-DAY BABY TUTORIAL
Hurley's Homestyle Kitchen • by Meg Maxwell
When FBI agent Colt Asher, who's been left with his baby nephews for ten days before Christmas, needs a nanny, he hires Anna Miller, a young Amish woman on *rumspringa* trying to decide if she wants to remain in the outside world or return to her Amish community.

#2585 HIS BY CHRISTMAS
The Bachelors of Blackwater Lake • by Teresa Southwick
Calhoun Hart was planning on filling his forced vacation with adventure and extreme sports until he broke his leg. Now he's stuck on a beautiful tropical island working with Justine Walker to get some business done on the sly—and is suddenly falling for the calm, collected woman with dreams of her own.

#2586 THEIR CHRISTMAS ANGEL
The Colorado Fosters • by Tracy Madison
When widowed single father Parker Lennox falls for his daughters' music teacher, he quickly discovers there's also a baby in the mix—and it isn't his! To complicate matters further, Nicole survived the same cancer that took his wife. Can Santa deliver Parker and Nicole the family they both want for Christmas this year?

YOU CAN FIND MORE INFORMATION ON UPCOMING HARLEQUIN® TITLES, FREE EXCERPTS AND MORE AT WWW.HARLEQUIN.COM.

HSECNM1017

Get 2 Free Books,

HARLEQUIN

SPECIAL EDITION

Plus 2 Free Gifts—
just for trying the
Reader Service!

YES! Please send me 2 FREE Harlequin® Special Edition novels and my 2 FREE gifts (gifts are worth about $10 retail). After receiving them, if I don't wish to receive any more books, I can return the shipping statement marked "cancel." If I don't cancel, I will receive 6 brand-new novels every month and be billed just $4.99 per book in the U.S. or $5.74 per book in Canada. That's a savings of at least 12% off the cover price! It's quite a bargain! Shipping and handling is just 50¢ per book in the U.S. and 75¢ per book in Canada.* I understand that accepting the 2 free books and gifts places me under no obligation to buy anything. I can always return a shipment and cancel at any time. The free books and gifts are mine to keep no matter what I decide.

235/335 HDN GLWR

Name	(PLEASE PRINT)
Address	Apt. #
City	State/Province	Zip/Postal Code

Signature (if under 18, a parent or guardian must sign)

Mail to the **Reader Service:**
IN U.S.A.: P.O. Box 1341, Buffalo, NY 14240-8531
IN CANADA: P.O. Box 603, Fort Erie, Ontario L2A 5X3

Want to try two free books from another line?
Call 1-800-873-8635 or visit www.ReaderService.com.

*Terms and prices subject to change without notice. Prices do not include applicable taxes. Sales tax applicable in N.Y. Canadian residents will be charged applicable taxes. Offer not valid in Quebec. This offer is limited to one order per household. Books received may not be as shown. Not valid for current subscribers to Harlequin Special Edition books. All orders subject to approval. Credit or debit balances in a customer's account(s) may be offset by any other outstanding balance owed by or to the customer. Please allow 4 to 6 weeks for delivery. Offer available while quantities last.

Your Privacy—The Reader Service is committed to protecting your privacy. Our Privacy Policy is available online at www.ReaderService.com or upon request from the Reader Service.

We make a portion of our mailing list available to reputable third parties that offer products we believe may interest you. If you prefer that we not exchange your name with third parties, or if you wish to clarify or modify your communication preferences, please visit us at www.ReaderService.com/consumerchoice or write to us at Reader Service Preference Service, P.O. Box 9062, Buffalo, NY 14240-9062. Include your complete name and address.

HSE17R2

SPECIAL EXCERPT FROM

HARLEQUIN®

SPECIAL EDITION

Ella Baker is trading music lessons for riding lessons from the wild twin McKinley boys—but it's their father who would need a Christmas miracle to let Ella into his heart.

Read on for a sneak preview of the RANCHER'S CHRISTMAS SONG, the next book in New York Times *bestselling author* **RaeAnne Thayne**'s *beloved miniseries* **THE COWBOYS OF COLD CREEK**.

Beckett finally spoke. "Uh, what seems to be the trouble?"

His voice had an odd, strangled note to it. Was he laughing at her? When she couldn't see him, Ella couldn't be quite sure. "It's stuck in my hair comb. I don't want to rip the sweater—or yank out my hair, for that matter."

He paused again, then she felt the air stir as he moved closer. The scent of him was stronger now, masculine and outdoorsy, and everything inside her sighed a welcome.

He stood close enough that she could feel the heat radiating from him. She caught her breath, torn between a completely prurient desire for the moment to last at least a little longer and a wild hope that the humiliation of being caught in this position would be over quickly.

"Hold still," he said. Was his voice deeper than usual? She couldn't quite tell. She did know it sent tiny delicious shivers down her spine.

"You've really done a job here," he said after a moment.

"I know. I'm not quite sure how it tangled so badly."

She would have to breathe soon or she was likely to pass out. She forced herself to inhale one breath and then another until she felt a little less light-headed.

"Almost there," he said, his big hands in her hair, then a moment later she felt a tug and the sweater slipped all the way over her head.

"There you go."

"Thank you." She wanted to disappear, to dive under that great big log bed and hide away. Instead, she forced her mouth into a casual smile. "These Christmas sweaters can be dangerous. Who knew?"

She was blushing. She could feel her face heat and wondered if he noticed. This certainly counted among the most embarrassing moments of her life.

"Want to explain again what you're doing in my bedroom, tangled up in your clothes?" he asked.

She frowned at his deliberately risqué interpretation of something that had been innocent. Mostly.

There had been that secret moment when she had closed her eyes and imagined being here with him under that soft quilt, but he had no way of knowing that.

She folded up her sweater, wondering if she would ever be able to look the man in the eye again.

Don't miss
THE RANCHER'S CHRISTMAS SONG
by RaeAnne Thayne,
available November 2017 wherever
Harlequin® Special Edition books and ebooks are sold.

www.Harlequin.com

Looking for more satisfying love stories
with community and family at their core?

Check out **Harlequin® Special Edition**
and **Harlequin® Western Romance** books!

New books available every month!

CONNECT WITH US AT:

Harlequin.com/Community

 Facebook.com/HarlequinBooks

Twitter.com/HarlequinBooks

Instagram.com/HarlequinBooks

Pinterest.com/HarlequinBooks

ReaderService.com

**ROMANCE WHEN
YOU NEED IT**

HFGENRE2017R